A FLUTTER OF WINGS

By the same author

Novels :
The Unfortunate Fursey
The Return of Fursey
Leaves For The Burning
No Trophies Raise

Plays :
Alarm Among The Clerks
The Lady in the Twilight

Local History :
Forty Foot Gentlemen Only

A Flutter of Wings

Short stories

by

Mervyn Wall

THE TALBOT PRESS   **DUBLIN**

First published   1974

© Mervyn Wall

ISBN 0-85452-092-9.

Printed in Ireland at Richview Press Ltd.
for The Talbot Press

for Aileen

The first of these short stories *They Also Serve* was published in 1940 in *Harper's* and in *The Capuchin Annual*. I am indebted to the latter for permission to republish it. The others were published between then and 1960 in magazines in Ireland, Britain, the United States and other countries. All have been broadcast over sound radio.

M.W.

CONTENTS

'They Also Serve . . .'   9

Adventure   18

The Hogskin Gloves   30

The Demon Angler   41

Cloonaturk   53

Age Cannot Wither   68

Leo the Lion   76

The Men Who Could Outstare Cobras   92

The Metamorphosis of a Licensed Vintner   106

'They Also Serve . . .'

ONE AFTERNOON a middle-aged man walked up to the gateway of Dublin Castle. He had such a smart way of walking and held himself so upright that the policeman on duty had touched his helmet respectfully before he noticed the little man's outmoded and shabby clothes. Mr. Carmody coughed nervously before he spoke.

'I beg your pardon. Is this Dublin Castle?'

The policeman stared down at him as if suspicious of a joke. 'Yes,' he admitted, 'it is.'

'I have an appointment with Mr. Watkins,' Mr. Carmody explained. 'Perhaps you would be so kind as to tell me where I would find him.'

The policeman looked him up and down and replied sternly:

'There are seven departments of government in the Castle and a staff of over two thousand.'

Mr. Carmody shifted nervously.

'He's in the Department of Fisheries.'

The policeman moved two paces and stood with his arm stretched out like a signpost.

'Go down there,' he said, 'across the Lower Yard, round by the Chapel Royal, and when you come up against a blank wall, turn to the left.'

Mr. Carmody began to thank him, but the policeman went on without heeding him.

'The Department of Fisheries is moving out today to another building, but you may get the man you're looking for if he hasn't left.'

9

Mr. Carmody thanked him again, crooked his umbrella on his arm and walked through the gates. He crossed the Lower Castle Yard, glancing up at the black battlements of the Wardrobe Tower. He turned the corner by the Chapel Royal, gazing with admiration at the Latin inscription over the doorway. He did exactly as the policeman had told him, and in a few minutes he came to a group standing round a door. Officials were hurrying in and out giving directions to some workmen who were loading filing boxes and bundles of papers on to a van. Mr. Carmody went up to some young men who stood with waterproof coats folded over their arms.

'I beg your pardon,' he said, 'could you tell me if this is the Department of Fisheries?'

'Yes,' answered one, 'but we're moving out to-day to make room for Internal Affairs. Were you looking for anyone in particular?'

'I have an appointment with Mr. Watkins,' explained Mr. Carmody.

'I don't know that he hasn't left. Try the second floor, turn to the right, and when you come to a fire extinguisher it's the third door on the left.'

Mr. Carmody thanked him and went in. He mounted two flights of stairs and, turning to the right, found himself on a landing from which he could see quite a number of fire extinguishers. He was standing in a narrow passage summoning up courage to enter one of the rooms when a door suddenly opened and out came a heavy table and pinned him to the opposite wall. From the other end of the table a workman's red face gazed across at him in astonishment. When Mr. Carmody was released he thanked the workman and knocked at the first door he came to. A voice said: 'Come in,' and Mr. Carmody hastily took off his bowler hat and entered. An elderly man was sitting at a table writing.

'Hello,' he said, 'have you come to move the safe?'

Mr. Carmody said he had come to see Mr. Watkins.

'I don't know that Watkins is in the building,' replied the elderly man. 'You see, we're vacating these offices. Is there anything I can do?'

Mr. Carmody coughed with some embarrassment. 'Well, it was about a post,' he said. 'I have been looking for a job for some time past, and someone, a friend of mine, spoke to Mr. Watkins, who wrote to me to call and see him.'

The elderly man looked at him severely.

'You can't get into the Civil Service that way,' he said. 'You must pass a qualifying examination and receive a certificate of appointment from the Minister. Besides, I doubt if Mr. Watkins —— he holds a comparatively junior position.'

'It wasn't a post in the Civil Service,' Mr. Carmody put in hurriedly. 'I thought he might know of something outside in the city. I thought he'd be able to give me some advice as to how I should proceed.'

The elderly man looked at Mr. Carmody for a moment. 'How old are you?' he asked.

'Forty-two.'

The elderly man seemed to become suddenly embarrassed.

'You'd better wait for Mr. Watkins,' he said.

He led the way to the door. Mr. Carmody took his umbrella and followed. The elderly man tried to bring Mr. Carmody up another flight of stairs, but he was prevented by two diminutive workmen who had got into difficulties with a large filing press at a place where the banisters curved.

'They're moving furniture,' said the elderly man. 'It's hardly safe to be out in the corridors.'

Mr. Carmody agreed with him.

'You'd better wait in here,' the elderly man said, leading the way to a room at the end of the passage. 'I'll send in Watkins when he turns up.'

Mr. Carmody thanked him and took the liberty of sitting down on the edge of a chair.

The room was small and ugly. There was a calendar on the wall with the day's date, 27th January 1922. The only furniture was the chair on which he was sitting, and a table littered with papers. Among them was a file of about forty typed pages of foolscap fixed together with a brass fastener. Mr. Carmody blew off the dust and read: 'Suggested Scheme for the Industrial Development of the Ballinacorrig Oyster Beds.' He turned the first page and began to read with mild interest.

An hour passed. He suddenly realised that everything was very quiet. He could no longer hear the workmen in the passages. He tiptoed to the door, opened it and put out his head. For some time he heard nothing, then he became aware of approaching footsteps, and a young man turned the corner and came down the passage reading a sheet of paper as he walked, so that he did not see Mr. Carmody until he was close by.

'Hello,' he said in a surprised voice when he saw Mr. Carmody's head. 'Are you waiting for someone?'

Mr. Carmody told him about his appointment.

'The Department of Fisheries has moved out,' said the young man, 'but, of course, if you have an appointment with someone, no doubt he'll turn up.'

He was a friendly young fellow with ginger hair, and he seemed to have time on his hands for he offered Mr. Carmody a cigarette and loitered round the room talking for a bit.

'I'm from Internal Affairs,' he explained. 'We'll be moving in this evening, and they sent me on in advance with a list of the rooms we're to occupy. That's in case the Department of Arts and Crafts tries to grab any of our rooms. They're in the same building, you see. They're extending, too. They're getting some of these rooms Fisheries were in.'

12

'I didn't know two Government departments were ever housed in the same building,' said Mr. Carmody.

'Oh, Lord, yes,' replied the young man, 'often. Just according as there's accommodation. In this building Arts and Crafts were all mixed up with Fisheries, one room one department, the next room the other department. They'll be all mixed up with us now.'

'A very remarkable system,' said Mr. Carmody.

'Ah,' declared the ginger-headed young man, 'what does it matter? We get to know our own rooms quick enough, and a stranger has only to enquire.'

'A country's Civil Service is a wonderful organisation,' said Mr. Carmody.

'Ay,' grinned the young man. 'You see, it's only a few weeks since the Irish Government took over from the British. That's why all this changing of buildings is going on. And there have been practically no hitches. The Civil Service isn't really such a funny institution as people make out. It's slow in its movements, but it's sure.' He went to the window. 'I think I hear the Board of Works men arriving with the furniture. I wonder is this room of yours on my list.' He opened the door. 'Number 107. No. Arts and Crafts must be coming in here.'

'I hope Mr. Watkins hasn't forgotten that he made an appointment with me,' said Mr. Carmody, 'I'm sure I've been waiting over an hour.'

The young man hesitated at the door. 'He may have been delayed, there's so much confusion to-day on account of the staff moving out. Might be worth your while waiting for a bit, that's if you're not in a hurry anywhere.'

Mr. Carmody assured him that he wasn't in a particular hurry anywhere and that he'd wait for another while.

'Good-bye now,' said the ginger-headed young man, and he went out.

Mr. Carmody sat down again and, resting his head between his hands, went on with his reading. He was re-perusing Section 23, which was not at all clear, when the trampling of feet and an occasional crash informed him that Government furniture was once more being moved. He continued to read until the sounds of activity came to the corridor outside. He listened for a while, and then as he was getting anxious lest Mr. Watkins had indeed forgotten him, he went over again and opened the door. Workmen were moving tables into the room next to his. An official stood alongside with a piece of paper and a red pencil in his hand. A workman came down the passage carrying a pile of papers.

'Arts and Crafts stuff,' he said.

'Right,' said the official. 'Bring them in.'

'What about the end room?' asked another, 'is there anything to go in there?'

The official read the number over Mr. Carmody's head: '107,' and he consulted his list. 'No, we're not getting 107. Internal Affairs must be moving in there.'

'That's all then?' asked the first workman.

'That's all,' said the official, and without as much as a glance at Mr. Carmody they all went down the corridor.

For a few minutes he stood in the doorway, then he stepped back into the room. 'That's queer,' he said to himself, 'this room is not on the Internal Affairs list and not on the Arts and Crafts list, and each of them thinks it belongs to the other department.'

He sat thinking what a great organisation the Civil Service of a country was, and yet how easily a mistake like that could be made. Then he sat for a long time watching the light fade out of the sky above the roof of a tenement house in Ship Street. It was growing late in the afternoon, the room was no longer light, soon it would be half dark. He knew suddenly that Mr. Watkins must have forgotten the appointment and that the right thing for him to do was to go away and call tomorrow at the new offices, wherever they were; but he found he was unwilling to go. His heart sickened when he thought of having to go out again into the chill fog of the city. He thought of the misery of his position, the heart-breaking search for a job, any job at all, and the interviews with successful patronising men, which were such a hurt to his shyness and his pride.

Christ Church Cathedral bell sounded its warning notes, and then it slowly struck the hour. Four o'clock. He remembered his miserable lodgings where there was no fire and where the rent was not paid. He thought of the misery of having to go on living at all. 'I'll stay till five when they all go,' he said to himself, 'at least there are hot pipes here and the room is warm.' He got up and groped for the electric light switch. He took off his overcoat and hung it behind the door. Then he seated himself at the table again with his head in his hands and forced himself to go on with his reading.

Half-past four had struck when he was surprised by a quick step in the passage and a knock at the door. A young man came in.

'Good evening,' he said briskly, laying on the table what seemed to be a list of names. 'I hardly know where I am with all this moving about of staff. What's your name, please?'

Mr. Carmody told him, and the young man added the name quickly to the list.

'I'll be round on the thirty-first about eleven,' he said. 'You'll be here about that time I suppose?'

'Here?' said Mr. Carmody.

'Yes, at eleven on Friday, the thirty-first. In this room.'

'Oh, you're from Mr. Watkins?'

'No,' replied the young man, looking puzzled, 'from Mr. O'Brien.'

'Oh,' said Mr. Carmody, not understanding a word.

'I'll always be here at eleven,' said the young man. 'Good evening,' and he went our briskly leaving Mr. Carmody gaping after him in astonishment.

*   *   *

On Friday at eleven o'clock Mr. Carmody sat in the room at the end of the corridor waiting for the young man to arrive. He did not understand why he was to be there, but he believed it was all connected in some way with the original appointment made by Mr. Watkins. The room was unchanged, the table was still littered with abandoned papers. At five past eleven the young man came in, brisk as before, with a bundle of paper slips in his hand.

'Good morning,' he said. 'Awful work we have over in Finance, what with the change of Government and the staffs moving all round the city. Your name is —— ?'

'Carmody,' said the other, wondering what was going to happen next.

'Benedict Carmody,' said the young man selecting a slip of paper from his bundle and laying it on the table. 'I'll be here at the same time on the last day of next month. Good morning.'

When the door closed Mr. Carmody gazed with amazement at the slip of paper. It was headed 'Department of Internal Affairs Vote' and it was a cheque for thirty pounds.

*   *   *

Mr. Carmody has now been in occupation of the little room for seventeen years. He comes in every morning about a quarter to eleven and reads the newspaper, then he looks at the ceiling and smokes cigarettes through a long holder until lunch time. He meditates at times on the vastness of a country's Civil Service and says to himself that it isn't such a funny institution as people make out. The 'Suggested Scheme for the Industrial Development of the Ballinacorrig

Oyster Beds' lies permanently on the table before him, lest by not appearing to be at work he should give scandal to anyone who may come into his room by mistake. He is very rarely disturbed, however, since in his second year he wrote 'Private' on a sheet of paper and pasted it on the door. He feels himself perfectly secure, as the officials of each department no doubt imagine he belongs to the other one whenever they chance to see him in the passages, that is if they think about him at all.

In the afternoons he usually goes for a stroll through the streets or sits in one of the city parks until the evening editions of the newspapers come out. Sometimes he takes a week's or a fortnight's holiday, but he is always careful to be back on the last day of the month to receive a brisk young man with a bundle of cheques.

He has six years to run before he reaches the retiring age. He is beginning to worry about whether they will give him a pension.

FW—2

Adventure

WHEN THE alarm clock began to ring at a quarter to eight George Drake clambered quickly out of bed to switch it off. You had to get up when it rang because it was one of those roundfaced alarm clocks which, on a smooth surface like a mantelpiece, are propelled forward by the excited motion of the hammer. Its predecessor had once nearly frightened the wits out of Mr. Drake by flinging itself on to the floor where it had careered round in circles on its face in an absolute fury.

'Are you up, George?' came his sister's voice from the neighbouring room.

He did not answer as he considered this a stupid question; instead he let up the blind and blinked out at the sunshine flooding his eighth-of-an-acre garden and the twenty-three similar gardens along the road.

'Are you up, George?' came the voice again, accompanied this time by determined knocking on the wall. He poured the water into the basin and reflected that there were few things in the world as irritating as a shrill woman. A moment later she put in her head.

'Oh, I didn't know you were up. I was afraid you'd be late for the office.'

'I'm up.'

'Happy Birthday.'

'Oh —— h, thanks.' He shyly rubbed the sponge across his jaws.

'I've left a little surprise for you downstairs.'

'Oh, Jane, you shouldn't have bothered.'

'Why not? You've only one birthday in the year,' and she smiled happily as she closed the door.

His mind was so occupied with the shame of being forty years of age that he cut himself twice while he was shaving. At the breakfast table he gravely simulated delight when he opened the brown paper parcel to find that the 'little surprise' was, as he had expected, the pullover she had been knitting for the previous seven months. He even tried to appear gratified when she told him she had invited Mr. and Mrs. Lyon to play bridge that evening. (Mr. Lyon was a hearty man who made puns.) 'Just a little celebration for your birthday.'

He was very preoccupied as he strode in his queer ungainly way past the suburban gardens towards the railway station. It was the first of May, and the birds were aware of it. He, too, was conscious of the rash yellow forsythia, the almond and the plum-trees in blossom already and the hawthorn doing its best. He felt the sunlight, but he was most of all aware of the little mocking winds that came around the corners stirring things.

Seated in the train he opened his attaché case and took out his book from its place beside his thermos flask, his package of sandwiches and his hard-boiled egg. It was *The History of Pendennis*, but he did not read it for long.

He was only at page 30, and a glance at the back made him wonder would he ever finish it. He looked out the window instead. Here and there the valerian had put out a purple flower, soon the whole embankment from Dalkey to Sandy-cove would be a crazy mass of colour. Quite involuntarily his favourite day-dream took possession of his imagination, and he saw himself in darkest Africa, an explorer painfully forcing his way through unmapped jungle with incredible adventures before and behind him. He pulled himself together suddenly and glanced sheepishly at his fellow-travellers. Really, how long had he being trying to break himself off that childish habit, twenty, twenty-five years?

When he emerged from the railway station he paused on Butt Bridge to look down the river. A cargo-boat was being loaded close at hand, and the shuffling and clanking of the cranes made a pleasant sound. Jersied sailors stirred lazily on the decks. Moving on across the bridge into the shadow of the Custom House he mounted the steps and went deeper and deeper into a dark labyrinth of corridors till he came to a small room. There he took out his fountain-pen and wrote '9.30. George Drake' in the attendance book. He went on upstairs then, saying 'Good Morning' to everyone he passed.

The room in which Mr. Drake worked was long and narrow. He occupied a table at one end and facing him sat the only person in the world over whom he exercised authority, a fat freckled youth from the provinces. At the far end of the room sat the Deputy Assistant Principal, who was in charge of the thirty-odd men and women in the Section.

As Mr. Drake entered he heard his freckled subordinate saying: 'Here's Slopey Joe,' but he pretended not to hear. He sat down and spreading his newspaper read it for the customary ten minutes. Then he lit his pipe and got out a return prepared the previous day. He laid it before him so as to be ready for the daily telephone call at ten o'clock from the Deputy Assistant Principal at the other end of the room asking for 'the figure'. That done, he glanced coldly at the freckled youth who was whistling a cavatina between his teeth, and settled down ceremoniously to work.

Shortly after eleven the staff was suddenly aroused by a blare of martial music from the quayside below. The Deputy Assistant Principal being out of the room, the whole junior staff rushed to the windows. Mr. Drake and the older ones moved after them, but with more dignity. A company of soldiers was marching by headed by a military band. A horde of excited street urchins marched alongside. The brass instruments flashing in the sun, the bayonets and the swinging leggings made a brave display. Mr. Drake's blood quickened to the music. He had turned to make a remark to someone at his elbow when he noticed that most of the staff were resuming their seats with an elaborate air of unconcern. The Deputy Assistant Principal was standing beside him looking down at the quayside too.

'That sort of thing must cost the Department of Defence a lot of money,' he remarked lightly to his superior.

'Yes, yes,' nodded the Deputy Assistant Principal vaguely, 'and it costs this Department a lot of money too.'

A hush fell upon the room. Every head was bent industriously as Mr. Drake awkwardly returned to his table. The Deputy Assistant Principal stood for a few moments longer watching the parade, then he too walked down the room to his place. There was silence, and the music faded into the distance.

Mr. Drake appeared intent of his work, but the real reason he rested his forehead on his hand was to hide the fact that his face was hot. He was filled with a fierce hurt at the indignity of the reproof, mild as it was, in front of the entire staff. He worked badly: again and again he went up and down a column of figures trying to find an elusive error. In the end he had to call in his freckled subordinate, who grinned inanely as he suggested that perhaps Mr. Drake was including in the tot the figure representing the date at the head of the column. At last one o'clock struck. It was Mr. Drake's usual practice to wander aimlessly about the streets for the first half of the midday interval and return to the office in time to eat his lunch before his colleagues came back, but to-day he found himself walking rapidly along the quays full of disgust for the system that compelled him to spend the whole of a bright spring day in a dreary room. A sudden idea struck him: he would take a bus out to the Park and have his lunch in the open air. Even if he was ten minutes late back it wouldn't matter. That was the best of having a reputation for punctuality; if you were late, everyone assumed it was absolutely unavoidable. He felt better when he had made this decision, and with sudden recklessness he stopped outside a cut-price shop. After all it was his birthday, he would buy some chocolate.

The shopkeeper was an irritable little man who was talking about the effect of the war on his business as he tied up a parcel of cheap soap for a poor woman who stood at the counter. As Mr. Drake waited to be served he gazed through the door at the posters outside a newsagent's on the opposite side of the street: 'Great Empires In Death Grips,' 'Bloody Encounters Along Thousand Mile Front.'

'The material isn't the same,' said the shopkeeper. 'Everything is rotten.'

The little woman murmured sympathetically.

The twine with which he was tying her parcel snapped suddenly. The shopkeeper breathed savagely through his nostrils.

'You see what you're up against,' he said fiercely and began a diatribe against the Government.

When the shabby woman was gone Mr. Drake bought three bars of chocolate. Leaving the shop, he held up his umbrella authoritatively and stopped a passing bus. He clambered jauntily on top and sat at the back so as to be able to bite pieces off his chocolate without being seen by the other passengers.

As he walked up the hill in the Park past the eighteenth-century fort some children at play left off their game to gape at the gaunt man with the queer sloping stride, but he did not even notice them. At the second turn on the road he found a seat that was an old favourite of his because of its commanding view of the river. Here he seated himself and glanced guiltily at his watch. Twenty minutes to two. With reckless abandon he thrust it back into his waistcoat pocket and with a smile that was almost wicked, he clicked open his attaché case. He ate rapidly all the same for he was afraid of being really late, and when he was finished he lit his pipe and decided to remain enjoying the view for five minutes. That should bring him back to the office before half-past-two. He saw quickly in his mind's eye a muttered excuse to his superior, an accident on the road, the bus running over a dog or something equally plausible.

It was a beautiful day, all about him the trees were covered with funny little buds for all the world like Brussels sprouts. Below him was a hollow with twisted hawthorns that reminded him of woods he had known in the fairy stories of his childhood. Beyond the wall of the Park the river wound between peaceful fields and bent out of sight among the trees.

Five minutes ticked away in Mr. Drake's waistcoat pocket, and yet another five; still he did not move. He was thinking how interesting it would be to follow the towpath along the far bank and find out what lay beyond the curve of the river. Indeed, he couldn't imagine anything in the world more pleasant than to wander along that river bank this afternoon.

In a sudden fright he looked at his watch: ten past two. He got up hurriedly and started back down the hill towards the city. He remembered that when he was a boy he had longed to be grown up because grown-ups seemed to be able to do what they liked. Yet when he was a boy there had been strange roads and lanes to explore and reasonable leisure in which to do it; one hadn't to spend one's day totting columns of other people's money and one's nights playing bridge with old crows. 'Old crows indeed!' he reflected bitterly: he was now middle-aged himself.

An exciting idea interrupted his reflections. At first he dismissed it as too outrageous, but it kept coming back to his mind and becoming more and more attractive. He came suddenly to a decision and stopped outside a telephone kiosk. At first he thought of disguising his voice as that of a maid-servant and saying: 'Mr. Drake regrets that he has been suddenly taken ill and will be unable to return to the office this afternoon,' but he concluded that his probable inability to sustain falsetto in the event of the conversation being prolonged by anxious inquiries, would give him away. Moreover, the Deputy Assistant Principal, in a fit of penitence over his unjust treatment of the sick man that morning, might take the afternoon off and turn up at Mr. Drake's house in Dalkey with a brown paper bag full of grapes. You couldn't be too careful in these matters. Instead, he told his superiors over the phone that his sister was very unwell and that he was unable to leave her. He gruffly acknowledged the polite enquiries at the other end of the line, hoping that the quaver in his voice would be taken for anxiety on his sister's behalf. Then with a sense of schoolboy excitement he crossed the bridge and, glancing to left and right to assure himself that there was no one he knew in sight, he left the road for the fields that led to the river.

He ambled happily along the water's edge, not dawdling, for this was a journey of exploration. The birds sang, the river moved sluggishly by, cattle raised their heads to watch him. He made a discovery about rivers: when walking along a river bank you should walk towards the sun, not with your back to it: a river looked ever so much brighter when you viewed it facing the light. Moreover, you should walk in the opposite direction to the course of the water so as to see and enjoy waterfalls all the time you are approaching them. If you walked downstream, you didn't see waterfalls until you came to them, and then you left them all too quickly behind.

When he had walked for about twenty minutes Mr. Drake was disappointed to find that he could continue by the water's edge no longer. A house and garden lay athwart his path, and the fields on his left ended at a wall. Would he have to retrace his steps? He was in no mood to be baulked by an eight-foot wall, and although hampered by his umbrella and attaché case he succeeded in mounting it and falling on his feet on the road on the far side. He inspected a tear in the knee of his trousers and spent a moment wondering how he would explain it to his sister. Then he dismissed the matter as trivial; the important thing was to find the river again. He walked down the road and on turning the corner found himself in the village of Chapelizod. He leaned over the bridge for a while and gazed sternly at the river which rambled with irritating unconcern between houses and gardens; but he wasn't by any means beaten: no doubt by continuing beyond the village he could rejoin it further on. He set out along the road, but he had to walk for a long time before coming to a low wall from which the river could again be seen. Although the wall on his side was low, there was a considerable drop into a field on the far side. About twelve feet, he thought; and he wondered would his legs stand the strain. He sat on the wall to see how it looked from there. Of course, he could drop his umbrella and attaché case first, and then he would have to go after them. Still, it would be no joke to have to lie at the foot of the wall for hours with a broken leg and maybe not be found before night came on. But the river looked so delightfully meandery between its fields of thistle and occasional trees that he felt he could not bear to abandon the expedition. Besides, he thought he could manage the jump. He took off his glasses and putting them carefully in an inside pocket, nerved himself to spring.

25

'Hey!' said a voice behind him. 'Hey, you!'

Mr. Drake relaxed his muscles and fishing out his glasses, put them on his nose. A policeman was standing beside him.

'What are you trying to do?' said the policeman. 'Commit suicide?'

Mr. Drake returned his gaze. 'No,' he replied.

'Turn round off that wall,' said the policeman, 'and tell me what you think you're up to.'

'My intention,' said Mr. Drake, 'was to get down to the bank of the river.'

'What for?' said the policeman quickly. 'Answer me. What for?'

'To walk along by the bank of the river.'

'Haven't you got the road to walk on? What do you think the County Council makes the roads for?'

'I prefer to walk by the river,' said Mr. Drake, who was becoming annoyed. 'I like rivers.'

'Ho,' said the policeman, 'you like rivers.' He looked at Mr. Drake for fully half a minute before playing his trump card: 'And have you the permission of the owner to trespass on his land?'

'If I had the permission of the owner, my entry on to his land would not constitute a trespass.'

'What?' said the policeman. He looked hard at Mr. Drake, then he knitted his brows very fiercely. 'What I'm tellin' you is that you have no right to trespass on private land.'

'You are being tautological,' said Mr. Drake. 'I have no right to trespass anywhere.'

The policeman seemed a little out of his depth. His eyes travelled all over Mr. Drake who tried to cross his legs nonchalantly so as to conceal the torn knee of his trousers.

'You'd better move along,' said the policeman at last. 'I don't mind tellin' you that I consider your behaviour is highly suspicious. Move along now.'

'Good afternoon,' said Mr. Drake picking up his attaché case and umbrella. The policeman walked slowly along the road after him as if to see him on his way. Mr. Drake's anger quickly evaporated. He remembered that he had recently read that the manners of policemen always deteriorate under a democratic form of government. It is far better to live under a monarchy if you have dealings with the police.

He walked for quite a long time without seeing the river again. He must have gone a couple of miles when he came on an individual of the tramp class sitting in the ditch grinning up at him. Mr. Drake stopped.

'I beg your pardon ——' he began.

'That's all right,' said the tramp.

'Maybe you could tell me,' said Mr. Drake, 'if this road joins the river again?'

'Fisherman?' asked the tramp.

'No,' replied Mr. Drake, 'and if it joins the river at what distance from here does that conjunction take place?'

'Not goin' poachin'?' queried the tramp.

'I asked you when the road joins the river again. If you don't know, please say so.'

The tramp rubbed his head. 'Just before Lucan,' he replied.

'Is that far?' asked Mr. Drake.

'Far?' echoed the tramp. 'Why, you're half-way.'

'Half-way from where?' asked Mr. Drake.

'Half-way from here,' said the tramp.

Mr. Drake looked hard at the tramp, who returned his gaze with great earnestness. The civil servant turned on his heel.

'You haven't a spare bit o' tabacca?' called the tramp after him, but Mr. Drake did not reply.

He walked on marvelling at the strange things that were happening to him this afternoon. No one would have imagined that there could be such quaint creatures in the world. That he had borne himself so well in each situation made him feel strong and self-reliant. With these thoughts he occupied his mind for another couple of miles until he came to a stretch of open ground beside the road, and there was the river once more. He wandered gratefully in among the weeds and furze and found a piece of grass beside the water's edge. Sitting there he gave himself up to his dreams, and soon his thoughts were in Africa. He saw himself again, as so often before, making that great trek from coast to coast, pushing on, the one white man in all that green hell. Sitting at his camp fire at night writing up his diary, he occasionally lifted his eyes to where his black boys were sitting at a respectful distance, or he paused to listen to the well-known sounds of the jungle. Tomorrow it would be necessary to begin making that circuit to the north to avoid the dangerous Monbuttu country. He could see that his boys were even already showing signs of uneasiness. Only the iron will of one white man kept them from breaking up and returning home. And then at last, when a rescue party was on the point of starting out to search for him, he staggered into the little trading town on the coast, his work done —— that vast territory between the head of the Congo and the Great Lakes mapped for the first time. He heard the shouts of the excited natives as they bore him through cheering crowds to the Residency, where the Resident and his lady waited on the verandah under white parasols to welcome him in the name of their government and, indeed, as the Resident so gracefully put it, in the name of all humanity.

A leaf fell from one of the trees on to the water. He started guiltily and looked at his watch. This time he was seriously alarmed, he would be late for the little bridge party Jane had arranged with Mr. and Mrs. Lyon. He scrambled to his feet and made out on to the road, asking himself bitterly why

Jane imposed these little parties on him. When he remembered that he was apparently not on a bus route and would have to walk to Lucan, he nearly broke into a trot.

Two hours later when he let himself into his house in Dalkey, his sister came out into the hall and told him through tight-set lips that the Lyons had been there a quarter of an hour. He apologised abjectly and tried to explain how it came about that he had been detained at the office. She cut him short and hunted him upstairs to change his torn trousers. Five minutes later he was shaking hands with the breezy Mr. Lyon. He took his place at the bridge table supperless, but smiling politely.

In the morning he arose at a quarter to eight when the alarm clock sounded, shaved, breakfasted and travelled by train to his work. He thanked those of his colleagues who enquired about his sister's health, and when, at ten o'clock the Deputy Assistant Principal rang up from the other end of the room for 'the figure,' he answered the phone in a voice resonant with integrity.

The Hogskin Gloves

WHEN A man has been eighteen years in the same grade and that grade the lowest in his Department, he gives up all hope of ever being promoted. That's the way it was with Joseph Demery. Those who had entered the Service at the same time as he, were now a rank or even two above him.

Again and again the lads had thanked some new promotee and accepted his invitation to come round after office hours to the pub at the corner. On these occasions Joseph would sit behind his pint of stout smiling happily at the sallies and at the buffoonery, while the lucky one stood with two inches added to his height magnanimously receiving the congratulations of each newcomer. The next morning Joseph would be back at the same desk, on the same hard chair on which he had sat for so many years, his blue eyes staring innocently across his ledger, out through the barred windows, at the great forty-foot wall opposite which kept the room in perpetual shadow.

It wasn't that Joseph wasn't a good official, he had the name of being a careful worker; but he was cursed with the vice of gentleness, and the rough country fellows who never accepted a reproof but argued the matter out with a superior even to the point of insubordination, had elbowed their way past him. When those in authority went gravely down the lists of possible candidates for a vacancy, they remembered the ones who had stood up to them, as being 'keen', as having strength of character and initiative, while Joseph who lost the power of speech when an official of higher rank spoke sharply to him, was passed over with a tick of the pencil.

As the years went by, his fellow-workers tended more and more to dismiss him with a kind word or two: 'Poor Joe Demery, a nice fellow. A great pity! So many years in the same job; ah, well, if he had been any good at all, he'd have been promoted before this.'

The staff called him 'Poor Old Joe,' not that he was really old—he was only thirty-eight—but those amongst whom he now worked, were much younger than himself. Moreover, years of stooping over a desk had rounded his shoulders, and the electric light playing all day on the top of his skull had discouraged the growth of his hair, which had become thin and scraggy; so that to the boisterous young men in Section N who listened tolerantly to his reminiscences of fifteen-year old events in the Department, he seemed a proper old fogey.

He lived within his means in a boarding-house on the South Circular Road, a grey, seedy house in which the only fire ever lit was an electric one plugged in grudgingly by the landlady at the beginning of each meal and carried away under her arm the moment the last boarder had finished his rice pudding. Joseph shared a bedroom with a chronic medical student who spent the greater part of his life in a public house and was therefore probably unconscious of the fact that a fire was never lit in the bedroom; but Joseph in his thin suit was very much aware of it, and as the only alternative during eight months of the year was to go to bed immediately after tea, it was his practice to leave the house every evening: on Mondays, Wednesdays and Fridays to go to a cinema, and on Tuesdays, Thursdays and Saturdays to drift round to some public house where he would often sit the whole evening over a pint or two of stout, hoping that someone would talk to him. On Sundays he took a tram across town to visit an aunt, his only living relative, a deaf and very fierce old lady who ruled an elderly maid and a parrot in a little brick house in Drumcondra and lived with the memories of a polite society of acquaintances long since dead.

Joseph got on well enough with the crowd in the boarding-house: two writing assistants from the Department of Finance, a bank clerk, a commercial traveller in a small way of business, a pimply young man connected with the grey-hound industry, the chronic medical student and, of course, Miss Barclay. They engaged in a little necessary conversation during meals, but otherwise had little to say to one another; certainly, each of them seemed determined to spend as little time as possible in the house. No sooner was a meal over than there was a general move upstairs for hats and overcoats. That is, all except Miss Barclay, who seemed often to have nowhere in particular to go. Sometimes when Joseph, returning at night from a cinema or a public house, let himself in through the hall-door, he would see, if the kitchen door at the end of the passage was open, Miss Barclay deep in a novel, her overcoat on, sitting on a chair beside the landlady, their knees up against the kitchen range where the last courageous spark was still fighting for its life.

Miss Barclay was a typist and was paid twenty-five shillings a week by the old, widely-respected firm of solicitors which employed her. Her family in Galway made her a small allowance and were becoming tired of having to do so, for they thought that a girl who had been fourteen years in the city, ought at least be able to earn her own living. She had told Joseph all about it years before in the days when the two of them used to linger on in the diningroom in conversation after everyone else had gone. They had been great friends then; and she had been the life of the house; but somehow, in recent years they had grown less intimate. She had become a quieter person, she no longer came down the stairs two at a time, her clothes were a little shabbier. Joseph often thought about it. He remembered particularly an evening four years before when the two of them had remained talking across the empty plates and the crumb-strewn tablecloth. She had been gaily tapping the soiled cups with a spoon trying to get a different note out of each, and she had asked him casually what his salary was. He remembered the way the light in her eyes had been suddenly extinguished.

It was the last day of the month, the day on which the great heart of the State gives a throb and sends millions of pounds circulating. There hadn't been much work done in the office that afternoon: conversation had been mostly about pints and about what part of the building, according to the latest telephone report, the cheque-man had now got to. At half-past five Joseph Demery made his way down the steps past the groups of animated civil servants; and now he stood outside Morrison's window where he had lingered every evening during the previous fortnight. Thirty-five shillings was a terrible price to pay for gloves, but he would certainly have to buy himself a pair; the old woollen ones he was wearing, darned by himself again and again, were really just too shabby. Of course, a pair of cotton ones would only be four-and-six or a pair of kids twelve-and-eleven; but that pair of yellow hogskins was really most enticing. On the other hand thirty-five shillings would leave him very short of money during the month. He walked slowly away from the window, but after going a few yards he halted and slowly drifted back. Thirty-five shillings . . . he could cut out some of the cinema shows and some of the evenings in the pubs. In any case he was beginning to drink too much. Some months previously the pimply youth from the boarding-house had introduced him to a small group of acquaintances that frequented the Stag's Head. There was a retired sea-captain who suffered grievously from the pangs of thirst, an ex-jockey

33

and a couple of others vaguely described as 'agents'. Joseph enjoyed these gatherings: everyone in the group spoke with authority on some subject or other, the sea-captain on the capacity of the standard Guinness barrel and on submarine warfare, the jockey was sure of a hearing when the conversation turned to the great world of sport, and he himself was listened to with respect when the talk was of the science of government. But these convivial evenings had their darker side. Thrice in the past month when he had found his way home, the hall-door had been bolted, and he had to fling handfuls of clay up at the window until at long last the chronic medical student had come unsteadily down the stairs and helped him up to bed, all the time lecturing him gravely on the evils of alcohol and telling him he was a disgrace. On the first occasion Joseph had been thoroughly ashamed of himself the following day: on the second occasion less so, and after the third distinctly self-satisfied. After all, Life was short and Youth was shorter. But in the office, gazing across his ledger through the barred window at the streak of sunlight on the great wall, he knew that he was foolish and that he was acquiring a taste for drink which he was just as well without, and he wondered how it was that in the evenings under the warm glow of the street lamps one looked at things so differently. It was this thought of his own deterioration that decided him. After all, if he spent thirty-five shillings now, he would have that much less money to drink during the month, which was all to the good. With a sudden spasm of recklessness he pushed in the door, apologetically stated his needs and in a couple of minutes was hurriedly stuffing the little parcel into the depths of his waterproof coat while he expressed his thanks to the indifferent assistant.

When he reached the boarding-house he went quickly up the stairs to his room. He locked the door and seating himself on the side of the bed he took out his purchase and examined it. They were a beautiful pair of gloves. They did not go on easily: you had to draw them on and they closed slowly over your hand with aristocratic disdain: but once on, they fitted you as if they had grown there. He marvelled at the softness of the material and at the two wicked-looking amber buttons. He fixed the mirror so that he could see himself, and then sauntered towards it, starting from the far wall with one glove off and held carelessly in the other gloved hand. Then he tried the effect of wearing both and permitting himself an airy gesture of two. In the diningroom below some surprise was occasioned by his absence from the tea-table . . . it was the first time for eighteen years that he had been late for a meal: and the boarders glanced occasionally at the ceiling and wondered at the sound of his erratic perambulations overhead. When he came down at last and took his place flushed and preoccupied, the chronic medical student looked grave and the landlady shook her head sadly. 'Mr. Demery has always been such a steady gentleman,' she told Miss Barclay that night over the kitchen range, 'I'd be real sorry if he was to get a taste for drink.' That night he entered the Stag's Head with such an air that the ex-jockey stopped short in a long rambling story of how a Colonel Slattery O'Callaghan had met a gentleman's death on the hunting field, and the hogskin gloves were passed around to be admired. The sea-captain immediately launched into an account of how he had hunted hog in Damaraland.

Joseph wore his new gloves every day, but he was still far from happy. The habit he soon acquired of taking a side glance at himself in the mirrors in shop windows made him acutely conscious of the deficiencies of his wardrobe. The pale yellow gloves were in alarming contrast to his stained and shapeless waterproof coat. Before the week was out he was standing in the evenings before lighted windows from

35

which waxen gentlemen in well-cut overcoats simpered at the passers-by. Eight guineas! Of course, it could be done, it would simply mean cutting out all cinemas and pubs for a couple of months. The best thing to do was to plunge, to walk right down on next pay-day and buy a coat, and worry afterwards about the extent to which you have left yourself short.

The purchase of an overcoat the following month changed his whole way of life. With three shillings in his pocket to last him thirty-one days cinemas and public houses were out of the question. The winds of March which raced through the streets of the old draughty city made his bedroom intolerably cold. There was only one refuge in the whole town . . . the National Library: and there he went. He was grateful for the warmth of the reading-room, but there was nothing he particularly wanted to read: he had long since grown out of the habit. He was embarrassed by the polite enquiry of the assistant. It was extraordinary: here was an affable young man competent to put a great deal of the world's knowledge before him, and he was unable to think of anything he wanted to know. At length he opted for 'something about the industrial history of Ireland'. He had heard one of his superiors using the phrase that morning, and he supposed it had something to do with the work of his Department. He was brought a pile of books on the eighteenth-century woollen trade.

The trouble about the overcoat was that he was unable to wear it. He was mortally afraid that a downpour of rain would put it out of shape: it had to hang in the wardrobe in the bedroom until the following month when he could afford to buy an umbrella. He foresaw too that his old hat and patched shoes would be absurdly incongruous, and he tried to forget that he needed a new suit and a few shirts as well.

Spring went and warm sleepy summer gave place to an interminable autumn, while month by month he painfully made his purchases. Each month it was the same: one day of excitement and satisfaction and four weeks of longing and dull routine. One November evening as he sat in the National Library dozing over *The Impact of the Industrial Revolution on Rural Ireland* (he had since read his way into the nineteenth century) it came to him quite clearly that he had set a ball rolling which he couldn't stop. He felt sudden alarm that he might never again see the interior of a cinema or converse with his friends in the Stag's Head. He would have to call a halt. He was a man and the master of his fate. After all, that silk dressing gown that he coveted, surely it could wait. Even the physical discomfort to which his clothes subjected him, seemed more than the human spirit could bear: since he had bought his new suit two months previously he had not dared to cross his knees for fear of spoiling the crease in his trousers. It was absurd; and it was high time he took one evening off. He rose from his place, carefully put on his stylish coat and the new green hat with the tiny peacock feather stuck in the band, and with an unaccustomed sense of freedom made his way out into the night air.

When he arrived at the Stag's Head he saw the ex-jockey and the sea-captain in their usual corner before two sloppy pints of stout. They had to glance twice before they recognised him.

'If it isn't the hard Joe Demery,' said the ex-jockey holding out a porter-moist palm to be shaken. Joseph removed his glove and shook hands with each.

'You look as if you had walked right out of the window of the Two Guinea Tailors,' said the ex-jockey by way of compliment. Joseph smiled diffidently and looked for a dry spot on the counter to hang his umbrella. Really, these were very vulgar fellows, and dressed like corner-boys.

'What are you havin'?' asked the sea-captain chinking a couple of shillings in his trouser pocket. 'I suppose the same old pint of plain.'

'Well no,' said Joseph, 'I think I'll have a whiskey.'

The sea-captain looked startled, then he slowly drew a coin from his pocket and ordered the expensive drink. They had a few more together, but the conversation languished. Joseph was very conscious of the shabby and world-battered appearance of his two companions, and he was uneasy lest anyone he knew should come in and see him with them. The ex-jockey, when it came to his turn to stand a round, slipped to the other side of the mahogany partition, and Joseph saw him in one of the mirrors counting his money. Then he came back and said he just remembered that he had an appointment. Joseph thought the whole affair very sordid, and when he left shortly afterwards he marvelled that he had at one time actually sought their company. Certainly, he wasn't going to be seen with them again. After all, if one wanted a drink, one should go to a hotel where one could at least drink in the company of gentlemen.

In the office his colleagues had got out of the habit of referring to him as 'Poor Old Joe'; indeed, the juniors now instinctively stepped out of his way in the corridors. The policeman at the gate always touched his helmet and said: 'Good-morning, Mr. Demery,' and Joseph graciously acknowledged the salute. Twice a Principal Officer joined him in the evening and walked down the street with him as far as the bus. On the first occasion terror clutched at Joseph's heart and he had been unable to formulate a suitable reply to the Principal's statement that it looked as if it were going to rain, but a fortunate distraction in the shape of a fallen cabhorse enabled Joseph to sketch the history of the horse-breeding industry in Ireland and express his fears for its future. 'A most interesting man,' said the Principal Officer to the Head of Division, 'a very serious student and, I understand, quite an authority in the domain of Irish industry.'

The junior staff rather foolishly based its hopes of promotion on the mild influenza epidemic which visited the city each winter, always imagining that some of the older officials in responsible positions were at last due for their eternal reward, not realising that civil servants who have breathed Government ink and the dry dust of documents for thirty years, gain an immunity from anything less virulent than the Black Death. But when at last a vacancy occurred, it was obvious to everyone that a man like Mr. Demery could not possibly be overlooked.

On the evening on which he was promoted, Joseph, on returning to the boarding-house, found Miss Barclay in the hall titivating herself in front of the mirror. Lately he always seemed to be meeting her, and when he told her of his good fortune she took him by the hands and congratulated him with evident sincerity. She was the life of the tea-table that evening, a veritable flashing mirror of girlish fun. After tea he remarked that he hadn't been at a cinema for ten months, and asked her diffidently would she care to accompany him to see 'Strong Man of the Rockies'.

When he proposed to her four months later she talked to him very seriously, telling him that a man of his education and abilities should not be content with his present rank, and suggested that he should have a man-to-man talk with his superior, pointing out that his was a keen and ambitious nature and that he was anxious to rise in the Service.

Miss Barclay certainly made a great success of the wedding. She insisted that the guests should wear top hats and morning coats, and she saw to it that there were photographers from all the newspapers. Several high officials of the Department had been invited, and there were four small girls scattering petals before the happy couple. The sea-captain and the ex-jockey stood round-eyed in the crowd outside the Church until the police moved them on. Everything went very well indeed, and even when the one contretemps occurred, that was during the breakfast when the chronic medical student fell under the table, the bride carried off the incident with a grace and charm that endeared her to everyone.

Since then Joseph Demery has been promoted again and again. Some tell you he owes his success to the drive and ambition of his wife, but others say you have only to look at the photograph in the papers last week when he was promoted to yet higher rank, to see the resolution and strength of character which is stamped on his face.

The Demon Angler

IT'S A queer thing. The visitors who come here are always full of talk about the 'other-worldliness' of Connemara. That's the expression they use—'other-worldliness'; I've heard them myself. You'll see them any day of the summer standing over there in the hotel garden, men and women in their strange tourist clothes, staring down at the sea and at the rocks and the islands, or across at the hills on the far side of the bay. They'll even stop you to ask whether the seaweed in Connemara is always of a saffron colour, and they'll tell you that saffron seaweed stretching three miles along the inlet, is a most remarkable sight. But what seems to impress them most of all is the roads in the neighbourhood when the night is coming on. Many a time a visitor in his new golfing jacket has joined me walking home in the twilight, and told me that he feels the 'other-world' is close at hand, that the air is tremulous and pregnant with something about to happen, and that he understands the Irish belief in a world of faery. I remember one gentleman referring to the whole area as 'The Haunted Coast'.

We never contradict the tourists. After all, they're a quiet, well-behaved class of people, and I suppose their holiday costs them a lot of money. Moreover, they provide us with a lot of interest and amusement during the summer, and God knows it's dull enough in a Connemara village; but we haven't the leisure ourselves for notions of that sort, about the 'other-worldliness' of the locality. You don't have time for that class of thing when you're trying to scrape a living from two acres of grass and rock, or from the uneasy sea. When I say it's queer this talk visitors have of a haunted coast, I don't mean it's queer that they should have such ideas—after all I wouldn't expect strangers to have the same way of looking at things as the normal people of the country-side—but it's queer in this way, that the only genuine authenticated haunting we know of in this part of Conne-mara, is done, not by a creature from the faery world or even a deceased local, but by the ghost of a tourist himself—a draper's assistant from Capel Street, Dublin, by the name of Ambrose MacGrath.

I met him the first morning he was here: he came over from the hotel to speak to me where I was leaning over the wall smoking my pipe and looking down at the couple of row-boats in the harbour. He was a lanky young fellow dressed in navy blue, with a white unhealthy face; and he had a way of throwing his long legs about when he walked as if the hinges in his knees were loose.

He told me that he had arrived the night before for a fortnight's holiday, which he was going to spend in fishing for trout. He had never fished before, but the previous week in Dublin he had bought a rod, some casts and twenty-four flies as well as a net on a stick for landing the big ones. He also had four books on trout fishing in his suitcase. The girl in the hotel had pointed me out to him as the only angler in the village, and she had advised him to have a chat with me about the lakes and streams in the neighbourhood.

All the time he was talking he kept glancing over his shoulder, up and down the street, as if this was the queerest place he had ever set his foot in. Perhaps I should have told you that our village is just a row of whitewashed houses facing the sea. It straggles up the side of a hill as far as the church, and there it stops. After that, for sixteen good miles until you come to Clifden, there's just the road, the rocky coast, the bogs and the mountains.

42

At last he asked me where the inhabitants were. He said he had been out already that morning and walked the length of the village. He had counted just over a hundred houses; but while there was the same number of dogs, one lying at the door of each house with its paws crossed, he hadn't seen a single human being. I explained that most of the people would hardly be up yet—it was scarcely ten o'clock. Of course, between ourselves, another reason why he didn't see anyone, is that we're a very well-bred village. I've heard that elsewhere in Ireland the people all come to their doors to look at a stranger. We'd never think of embarrassing a visitor like that—our people watch a stranger from behind the curtains until he is out of sight.

Mr. Ambrose MacGrath was depressed because when he arrived the night before, the first thing he learned was that this isn't a trout fishing area at all, but a centre for sea-fishing. There were two English gentlemen staying at the hotel, one of them no less than a lord; and in the usual friendly Irish fashion MacGrath had opened his book of flies on the diningroom table and started to chat about the fishing prospects. They had kept themselves very aloof and had given him to understand that they were there to fish for Blue-nosed Shark, which are very plentiful off this coast. Later he saw the English lord coming through the yard carrying a twelve-inch hook on his shoulder—our friend thought at first it was a ship's anchor. That seems to have finished him. He slipped his little book of flies into his pocket and crept upstairs to bed.

While he told me this he kept staring at me with what I can only call resentment.

'I've always understood,' says he 'and the tourist literature that I've read, would seem to bear it out, that every bit of water in Connemara is leppin' with trout just dying to be caught.'

'I don't know how things may be in other parts,' I said, 'but to say that would be to exaggerate the position here. The fact is people just don't come here trout fishing at all. But you needn't be discouraged,' I added seeing how savage he was looking, 'there's two little lakes up the road beyond the church full of small trout, and in the bogs behind Errisbeg Mountain there's more lakes than you can count, and the trout there are large. I've fished every lake behind Errisbeg when I was a younger man, and you'll get plenty of sport there, tho' a city man like yourself may find it a bit wet underfoot.'

He cheered up considerably.

'I don't mind getting my feet wet,' says he. 'I brought plenty of pairs of socks with me,' and he explained that he was an assistant in the drapery business.

'I don't think you'll do so well to-day,' I said. 'The wind is in the north.'

He threw a queer look at me, and pulling a book out of his pocket he turned the pages until he came to a piece of poetry which he read half to himself and half to me:

> When the wind is in the north
> The wise angler fares not forth.

He began to look down-in-the-mouth again until I reminded him that as he had never fished before he couldn't do better than spend his first day in the hotel garden practising casts. We went up there together, and I showed him how to tie on the flies and how to flip his wrist. I must say he was an apt pupil, and he did no damage except occasionally to whisk a piece of the hotel laundry off the clothes line. After a time the proprietress came out and asked us would we mind practising somewhere else. So along we went to the first lake beyond the church, and even though the wind was in the north we tried our hand there. He didn't

44

catch anything; but I like to remember how happy he was that day walking back with me to the village. I think it was the only time I ever saw him happy.

The following day there was a thunderstorm, and of course that's ruinous—the trout just go to the bottom for a couple of days and bury their heads in the mud. After that the wind shifted to the east, and as one of his books told him that such conditions are 'neither good for man nor beast' Ambrose MacGrath didn't go out at all: he spent his time practising casts on the bit of waste ground down by the harbour, with all the children in the village lined along the wall watching him. Every now and again he'd gather a handful of grass to throw up in the air so as to find out whether the wind was changing to a more favourable quarter. This amused the children, and soon they were all at it.

I remember that it exasperated him greatly when every evening after sunset the English lord and his friend would come into the harbour with the couple of shark they had caught, and have them heaved up on to the pier to be measured and weighed. They'd leave them there for an hour or so to be admired by everyone before throwing them back again into the water.

I think it was on the Saturday that Ambrose MacGrath was in my garden complaining bitterly that half his holiday was over, when he suddenly discovered that the wind had changed. 'When the wind is in the south,' says he, 'it blows the hook in the fish's mouth,' and off with him like a shot to the hotel to get his tackle.

But he wasn't content even then; he was annoyed at the fine weather: it irked him particularly that fish won't rise when the sun is in the sky. 'I'm expected,' he said bitterly, 'to creep out like a malefactor in the early morning or in the evening when the sun has gone down.' What matter but he always spoke as if I was personally responsible for the vagaries of nature. I'm a peaceful man, but when he'd sit there in my kitchen uninvited, and look at me with real hatred, it used rise my dander to think of this city shop-assistant who wasn't content to behave like a normal fisher-man, but had such a mania for catching things. There almost at his door were two small lakes to wander round, rocks to scramble over to his heart's content, water to cast his flies in, and plenty of dry places to sit down and smoke his pipe. But no, he wasn't content: nothing would do him but he must catch a fish. I remember an evening he came in when I was sitting by the corner of the fire reading my way through the works of Sir Walter Scott, who must be the greatest writer in the world. I never saw a man that looked so black.

'There's a swan nesting on the lake,' says he.

'Well?' said I.

'Well indeed!' says he. 'How can I fish there? Every time I approach the edge the male bird comes rushing at me flapping its wings and disturbing all the trout.'

'There's the other little lake beyond,' I said.

'I can't get at the water there,' he says. 'There's ten yards of reeds all round it. I've lost five flies already.'

'Well,' said I, 'there's no use accusing me. I didn't make the country hereabouts.'

'I'm not accusing you,' he said very hot. 'I'm accusing Connemara,' and he muttered something about taking up the matter with the Tourist Board.

Seeing how put out he was I began to be sorry for him, so I promised to take the day off on the morrow and bring him up over Errisbeg to the great country of lakes beyond.

It was a nice cloudy day with the wind inclining to the west when we climbed the shoulder of the mountain and looked down at the three hundred and sixty-five lakes that are said to be in the twelve square miles of bog behind

46

Errisbeg. He was excited at first, but when we started the descent he began complaining again.

'I didn't know you were going to lead me into a morass,' he says as he sank to his knee in the bog.

'If you exercised more judgment as to where you placed your feet,' I replied, 'you wouldn't get so wet. Can't you walk where the ground is firm, and jump from tuft to tuft like I do?'

He wasn't much good at that either, and he was thoroughly wet when we scrambled down to the edge of Lough Nalawney, but the sight of the stretch of water brightened him up, and he had his rod fixed in a jiffy. Then he started bothering me as to what flies he should use. I always employ live bait myself. I kept flies at one time, but every winter the moths used eat them. At last he tied on a Wickham's Fancy and two other flies so brightly coloured that no trout would take them into his mouth except through wanton curiosity.

We fished the lake for a few hours, but when we sat down for something to eat he was at it again. He was a bit annoyed, I think, because I had taken a two-pounder while he had caught nothing.

'Look here,' says he. 'We'll say this lake is about a mile in circumference.'

'Right,' I said prepared to concede anything.

'The fishing books,' says he, 'tell you that you should only fish the leeside of a lake. That reduces the length of shore that you can fish from, to about a third of a mile.'

'Well?' I said. 'What about it?'

'Of that third,' says he, 'the greatest part is taken up by reeds which you can't cast across or by boggy soil which prevents you approaching the water's edge. So it amounts to this, that in a lake of this size there are really only five or six places from which you can fish at all. And to make matters worse,' says he, 'they tell you that you must cast with the wind. That's impossible,' says he, 'because if you're on the leeside of the lake the wind is blowing in your face. The whole thing is a cod,' says he. 'It's impossible to catch fish. It's all a device to defraud tourists.'

'No doubt you're right,' I said putting the two-pounder into my bag. That annoyed him more, and I left him muttering to himself, and off I went to have a cast or two myself. I took three more small ones while he didn't even get a rise tho' he tried every fly in his repertoire. When I joined him again he looked sourly at my take, and pulling out a map he screwed at it for a minute or two. Then he said he was going across to Lough Rannaghan. I tried to dissuade him—it was about a mile away across the bogs, and it's easy enough to get lost in that waste bit of country, especially with the evening coming on. But nothing would do him but to try his luck over there. I heard afterwards that he was out all night and with no luck either.

I didn't see him for a few days after that, but I heard from the girl in the hotel that he had written to Dublin for a pair of waders and a fresh consignment of flies of every known pattern. He hadn't a single trout to his credit yet and had become so short-tempered that everyone in the hotel was afraid to speak to him. Each evening he was off across the mountain, fished all the night through and returned to the hotel for breakfast. Then he went to bed to sleep or to read more books dealing with the psychology of the trout, which were arriving for him by every post. The girl in the hotel complained of the mess he had his room in, casts steeping in the water jug and the like; and she said that she couldn't make his bed or touch any of his clothes, even his pyjamas, without getting a hook embedded in her hand. I think the hotel people were looking forward as much as I was to the day when he'd return to his counter-jumping in Capel Street,

Dublin, but I declare to goodness on the Saturday there he was at my gate with a rod in his hand and a circle of flies around his hat.

'I got a rise last night,' he said with a glitter in his eye. 'At Lough Nalawney.'

'Did you now?' I said. 'That's very encouraging.'

'He took it into his mouth,' says he, 'but he spat it out again before I could strike. I think he must have been a big one by the force he employed in spitting out the fly.'

'Too bad,' I said, 'that you must return to Dublin to-day or to-morrow.'

He threw a crafty look at me. 'I'm not going back,' he says. 'I'm staying another week.'

'But what about your job?' I asked.

'I've a pain in my chest,' says he. 'I've been up to see the doctor, and he's given me a certificate. I've just posted it on to the firm.'

The month of August passed. Every week Ambrose MacGrath was up to the doctor. Poor old Doctor Maguire was sorely puzzled. He couldn't find anything wrong with MacGrath, but he had to take the patient's word for the pain. To make it more difficult the pain kept moving. The doctor followed it from MacGrath's chest round to the small of his back. It was six weeks later that the drapery firm in Dublin gave MacGrath the sack.

He didn't mind: he hadn't caught a trout yet, and he was now spending eighteen hours out of twenty-four at Lough Nalawney. Anxious and bitter letters kept arriving from his wife. He left them lying round the hotel so that soon the whole village knew that the wife and children had to leave their home because he wouldn't pay the rent. All his money went to buy a new rod, whole parcels of books on the life history of the trout, cases of flies and an extraordinary new suit of the colour and texture of grass.

'Have you ever studied background?' he says to me when he came in to show me the new suit.

'I beg your pardon,' said I.

'I know now,' he says, 'the reason for my lack of success. I've been reading all about background. The eye of the trout distinguishes sharply between colours, and if he sees a bit of navy blue moving against a background of green, he knows there's something up. You have to merge into your background. At Lough Nalawney the background is mostly long unhealthy looking grass. This is the nearest I could get to it in a suit. What do you think of it?' He turned round so that I could admire the back.

'It's like what the farmers call "silage",' I said. 'It's like a haystack only that it's green.'

He began telling me how he'd start fifty yards from the edge of the lake and crawl through the grass so quietly that the fish would think he was a bit of the bank. I listened, but all the time I was thinking of the wife and children without a roof over their heads, and the vacant place behind the draper's counter. He went on to tell me of a cannibal trout, a monster of about twenty pounds, that he had sighted sunning itself in the shallows at the edge of Lough Nalawney. For a solid hour he had held a Wickham's Fancy within an inch of its nose. Four times the trout had opened its mouth, and MacGrath had nearly fallen into the lake with the excitement. The fifth time it opened its mouth it came to him suddenly that the fish was only yawning, and in spite of the agonising pains he was suffering in his right arm he had tried to flick the fly down its throat, but the monster had turned and darted away into deep water. But he wasn't discouraged. He was determined to catch that particular trout, and he wasn't going to leave the village until he had it landed.

The people here considered him a bit cracked, but they didn't pay much heed, because they knew that all tourists are

50

queer; and none of us began really worrying about him until his determination to merge into his background made him paint his face and hands green. It was late in September, and tho' he still hadn't caught a single fish, he had twice sighted the same monster trout in Lough Nalawney. He had got it into his head that the other fish which jumped in the lake, did so to distract his attention from the pursuit of this grandfather of all the trout, and I believe that even if he had succeeded in catching any number of smaller ones, he wouldn't have been satisfied. No one ever went with him on his nightly journeyings across Errisbeg, and I don't blame them: I wouldn't have cared to go myself, keen angler tho' I am. It's a lonely spot to be with a fellow the like of that, a place where you wouldn't even have the company of your own shadow until the moon came up over the bogs.

After he painted himself green a few of us met one evening in the Atlantic Bar to talk it over and discuss whether we shouldn't start doing something about it. We thought of going up to the priest's house and asking Father James to talk to him. But we were too late: the following morning MacGrath didn't come back to the hotel, nor did he come during the day; and it was just coming on for nightfall when we found him. He had caught the monster trout, or maybe I should say that it had caught him. It had pulled him in. What grappling in the water up and down the lake the two of them had, no one will ever know. We found him drowned in the reeds with the twenty-pounder on his line.

It was a great sin he had committed against his wife and children, and no one can say but that he deserved his punishment. Maybe it was allowed to happen as a warning to the desperate fishermen you sometimes meet, who knows? Everyone spoke bad of him: I was the only one that tried to say a good word, because I'm an angler myself, and I know what it is when it gets its grip on you.

51

It wasn't long until stories began to be whispered round the neighbourhood, and soon it came to be thought unlucky for anyone, above all for an angler, to go near Lough Nalawney. First, a man herding his sheep across the side of Errisbeg saw from a distance something moving among the rocks beside the lake. Then there were others.

I know for myself, tho' I'm as mad about fishing as any man, I content myself with the two small lakes beyond the church. Nothing in this world would make me cross the ridge of Errisbeg of an evening. It's a ghostly place, Lough Nalawney, with no sound except the breeze stirring the grass among the rocks at the water's edge. Go and look at it yourself, but go in the day time when the sun is high over the bogs, and don't let anything on this earth persuade you to loiter there when it comes on towards evening and the sun goes down.

Cloonaturk

IF YOU travel the ups and downs of one of the little roads that goes west from Galway, and follow it as it worms its way into the depths of Connemara, you may at last come to the townland of Cloonaturk. You may, but it's unlikely; for there are no signposts and the inhabitants of these parts have an instinctive distrust of strangers, whom they invariably misdirect. Why, I cannot say. Maybe it's that they have no recollection of a stranger having ever conferred a benefit on them, and that they deem it wiser to be on the safe side by hurrying a stranger out of the neighbourhood by the shortest possible route. And even if you do come to Cloonaturk, you're as likely as not to pass through without realizing that you've reached it.

Cloonaturk is just thirty scattered cottages on a wrinkle of stony hill which creeps back from the sea towards the Maamturk Mountains. There's the same crazy-patterned landscape—the walls of loose stones zig-zag all over the place dividing the pale green fields which look no bigger than pocket handkerchiefs. The smallness of everything, the fields, the walls, the roads and the cottages, makes the arc of the sky seem immense, piled high as it usually is, cloud upon cloud. Round the bend of the road the grey Atlantic comes creeping in across the stones. Connemara is not like a part of this world at all, but like a locality which has strayed from a fairy tale. You would easily miss Cloonaturk; as I say, it's only thirty scattered cottages in a waste of rock and bog, hidden away in a corner of the inlet-worried coast. Even if you were to ask one of the inhabitants if this was Cloonaturk, it's doubtful if he'd do more than take his pipe from his mouth, regard you mournfully, and replace the pipe between his teeth.

The population seems to be made up of gaunt, silent, dreamy-eyed men of uncertain age, who meditate every question put to them, but rarely are able to rouse themselves sufficiently to give an answer. There don't seem to be any women, though there's a tradition that there were children once, but that they all emigrated to America.

Since the sixteenth century the inhabitants of Cloonaturk have subsisted entirely on a diet of poteen and potatoes. Poteen is of course an illicit drink; and its distillation should be suppressed by the authorities; but the police have long since given it up as a bad job. The slow-moving inhabitants of Cloonaturk have baffled every excise officer since the reign of George the First, and in the face of this tradition and after seven inglorious raids, the Sergeant in whose sub-district the townland lies, abandoned the matter as hopeless. 'Every man and dog in that place,' he declared bitterly, 'has his inside rotted through and through by reason of the consumption of illicit liquor.'

The inhabitants of the townland have always had a deep distrust of officialdom. It had been their experience for centuries that when an official began to take an interest in them, he had never anything good in his mind. He usually wanted money, and it took a long time to explain to him that nobody in Cloonaturk had any money. The inhabitants had of course heard of money; some of them had even seen it and could describe it: but none of them had ever handled it. And even if an official wasn't intent on being given money, he was as likely as not to have a dozen uniformed police hiding round the bend of the road; and those lads, you might be sure, were up to no good. They invariably had an assortment of probing rods and spades, and they were quite prepared to spend days wasting their own and everyone else's time digging up half the hillside looking for illicit stills which the inhabitants knew were somewhere else. The official mind was past understanding, and Cloonaturk took a very poor view of it.

It is therefore not surprising that one afternoon when a postman propped his bicycle against one of the loose stone walls which border the road, and came wearily up the track towards Pat's Tommy's cottage, the owner bolted the door and dragging his trestle-bed across the floor, began to barricade himself in. He had just removed his one cup from the dresser to a place of safety, preparatory to moving that article of furniture into position as well, when his eye fell on a long official envelope which had been pushed under the door. He heard the postman's retreating footsteps and realized that he had been outwitted.

For a long time Pat's Tommy stood motionless, gloomily contemplating the envelope; then he slowly shoved the bed back into its accustomed position against the wall, and taking the cup in one hand, he rooted with the other in the heap of peat piled high in the corner. He drew a bottle from its hiding-place and filled himself a cupful of poteen. Late into the night he sat drinking by the fire, filled with the gloomiest forebodings. The following morning he found it necessary to leave the cottage to bring in some potatoes. The unopened letter still lay on the earthen floor. After some hesitation he lifted it gingerly and placed it on the dresser. It remained there unopened until one evening four days later when, smiling slyly, he took it down, tiptoed over to the fire and burnt it.

He went about the little business of his acre of land in melancholy serenity until a week later the arrival of a second letter threw him into the utmost confusion. This time he did not hesitate, but seizing the envelope he thrust it into the heart of the glowing peat. But his peace of mind was now gone: a deep depression settled on him, and he waited fatalistically for the arrival of a third letter. It came on a grey afternoon when the soft, thin rain was falling. The words 'FINAL NOTICE' were stamped on the outside in broad red letters. Pat's Tommy sat on his stool the whole night through while the fire flamed and glowed and died. He emptied one bottle of poteen and made respectable inroads into a second. About an hour before dawn he sighed, and opening the letter, drew out a printed form. On one side there was a demand for the immediate payment of seven shillings and sixpence for a Dog Licence. On the back in small print were paragraph after paragraph of extracts from Acts of Parliament and a horrifying list of penalties. Pat's Tommy read it all through, finished the bottle of poteen, and went out into the barn and hanged himself.

Cloonaturk received its first intimation that something was wrong when a couple of days later three motor-cars suddenly appeared out of nowhere. Two small gentlemen with hard hats clambered out of one, and the others disgorged uniformed police and two loose-limbed individuals with hard faces, who immediately pulled out notebooks and started asking everyone questions. It was a fine, sunny morning; and the inhabitants had been mooching about their fields or leaning across the walls smoking their pipes and staring at nothing. Most of the inhabitants did not stay to be questioned: at the first sight of uniforms they hurried back to their respective cottages. But the police manifested exceptional determination and insisted on the arrest of twelve men. When they had twelve, they seemed to be satisfied.

Old Thady, who had a back door to his cottage, managed to make a getaway and fled up the hillside, but he was quickly overtaken and brought back. He was told that he was to be 'foreman', whatever that might mean, and he was placed carefully in the first car. The other eleven were packed in somehow, and the three cars started off down the winding road. They travelled for miles until they came at last to the old disused schoolhouse near Cashel. It was the first time that any of the inhabitants had been in a petrol-propelled vehicle, and they didn't like the experience. Indeed, Old Thady at one point tried to fling himself out, and would have succeeded only that one of the policemen happened to be sitting on his coat-tails.

When the old schoolhouse was reached, the twelve Cloonaturk men were ordered out and shepherded inside. They were put to sit on a long bench against the wall, and each one was presented with a notebook and pencil, which, having examined, they stowed away carefully in their tail-pockets. The first indication they had of what it was all about, was when the two hard-featured detectives at the door suddenly took off their hats, and Pat's Tommy was carried in on a shutter. The Cloonaturk men stared. It was true that no one had seen Pat's Tommy for a couple of days, but that was in no way unusual in Cloonaturk, where if a man felt like doing a little really serious drinking, he might retire to his cottage for a week. Their first thought was that the officials had murdered poor Pat's Tommy, but none of them ventured to speak. With such a crowd of officials present, the man who first opened his mouth might well be the next to share Pat's Tommy's fate.

What followed was a nightmare. One of the gentlemen climbed into the school rostrum and from there shouted at the twelve Cloonaturk men until he was crimson in the face. When he was exhausted, the Sergeant took up the shouting. The jury sat staring impassively at whoever happened to be shouting at the time, only manifesting interest when the other hard-hatted gentleman, who was apparently a doctor, suddenly hung a tube out of his ears and with the other end of it started tapping Pat's Tommy all over. It took two hours' shouting at the Cloonaturk men before it was slowly borne in on them that poor Pat's Tommy had done away with himself. They said nothing, but none of them blamed him. It's usual in many parts of Connemara to 'hang a dog against the licence'; that is, if you haven't got the seven-and-six, the only thing to do is to hang the dog. But it was remembered that Pat's Tommy had been fond of the little mongrel, so that his substitution of himself was not considered remarkable.

When the Cloonaturk men realized that none of them was going to be put into gaol on the head of Pat's Tommy's behaviour, they brightened considerably. They nodded their heads when the Sergeant instructed them to do so, and they crowded round to watch Old Thady make his mark on a document which the gentleman in the rostrum passed down to him. The Sergeant witnessed Thady's mark, and the proceedings terminated. The coroner gathered his papers, scowled at the Cloonaturk men, and stumped out of the schoolhouse. They were shepherded once more into the waiting motor-cars and conveyed back to Cloonaturk, where the remains of Pat's Tommy were surrendered to his friends.

The community breathed with relief when the last car disappeared over the shoulder of the hill. Their experience was too recent to admit of conversation, so after standing about for some time in silence, they bore Pat's Tommy awkwardly to Old Thady's house, which, on account of its possession of a back door, was regarded as the most considerable residence. Then they dispersed so as to give Old Thady some hours to prepare for the wake, and one man set out to tramp five miles to the nearest church to inform the Parish Priest that Pat's Tommy was coming along in the morning to be buried.

It was a powerful wake. Old Thady, perhaps on account of his failing eyesight, distilled a poteen that can only be described as vicious. When you took a gulp of it, you could feel the flame striking the pit of your stomach and then forking down each of your legs. While you were wiping the tears from your eyes, you felt your toes opening and shutting. But in spite of the potency of the liquor the men were silent, each slowly turning over in his mind the day's experiences.

On the morrow a little procession of middle-aged men in nineteenth-century tail-coats started along the five-mile road to the churchyard. Pat's Tommy went before on an ass-cart with two men sitting on the coffin.

When the last respects had been paid, the inhabitants of Cloonaturk streamed back, some singly, some in little groups. No one spoke, but with one accord they climbed the track to Old Thady's cottage, in which there was still a large quantity of poteen undrunk. The resumed wake lasted four days. On the second day there was some conversation of a monosyllabic character. On the third day there was some hard cursing as the twelve jurymen began to indicate to one another what they thought of their outrageous kidnapping by the police. From time to time a man fell asleep in an upright position leaning against the wall, and only awakened when someone fell over his feet. The one who had fallen, usually went to sleep where he lay; while the other who had been awakened helped himself to another drink. Occasionally someone said good-bye to his host and left by the back door, but on making his way round the cottage would find himself at the front door again. Realizing that there was a wake in progress, he would enter and remain for another twenty-four hours.

Long Joe Flaherty, a sad-eyed man with a drooping, black moustache which he had inherited from his father, was the first to get away from the cottage, which he did by slipping in the mud outside the door and rolling twenty yards down the track. He sat up on the ground and looked back at the house with a sense of satisfaction. He distinctly recollected having taken his departure no less than three times, but each time finding himself by some magic back inside the kitchen again with a cup of poteen in his fist. He got carefully to his feet and making his way to the road, screwed up his eyes and searched the sky to see where the sun was. At first he couldn't find it, but at last he discerned it over on his right half-way into the red Atlantic. Therefore it was evening. With a slow lumbering gait he started home. As he crossed the little bridge where the stream comes tumbling down between the stones, a familiar figure turned the bend of the road and came towards him.

'Good evening to you, Long Joe,' it said as it passed.

'Good evening, Pat's Tommy,' he answered and continued on his way.

He trudged on round the turn of the road and slowly climbed the track to his own cottage. It was only when he was taking off his boots to go to bed, that he remembered the man who had bid him good evening on the road.

'Strange,' he said to himself. 'I had an idea that Pat's Tommy was dead.' But the matter was too complex for further thought. He remembered that he had four nights' arrears of sleep to make up, so taking off his cap he hung it on the bed-knob and clambered into bed.

When he awoke it was midday. He lay for a long time on his back gazing at the ceiling. At last he struggled out of bed on to the floor and poured out a half-cup of poteen so as to steady himself. Then he went to the door and opened it, stepped out to see what sort of a day it was.

The sky was speckled with vagrant clouds. The mild sunlight lay everywhere; the air was clear. Long Joe's gaze wandered across the tumbled hills and came at last to rest on a small white cottage perched on the rising ground some four hundred yards from where he stood. It was Pat's Tommy's cottage, and as Long Joe gazed idly at it, the door opened, and out came Pat's Tommy with a spade on his shoulder. He was preceded by the little mongrel dog jumping and fawning on its master. Its joyous barking came across the fields through the thin, sunlit air.

Long Joe stood staring, then he turned quickly and re-entering the kitchen, poured himself another drink. Then he went out and had another look. There was no doubt about it. Pat's Tommy was assiduously digging in the potato patch at the back of the house. Long Joe retreated precipitately into his kitchen. Afternoon deepened into evening, and still he sat sipping poteen and staring vacantly in front of him, only stirring from time to time to brush from his moustache with a mechanical hand the little colourless beads of liquor.

Pat's Tommy's cottage was on a height clearly visible from all parts of the townland, so that Long Joe was not the only one who saw Pat's Tommy moving about the fields in his usual way, apparently unaware that he had been sat upon by a coroner and subsequently buried. 'Someone should tell him,' suggested Old Thady that night as the inhabitants sat in their usual meeting-place in the shelter of a bank at the crossroads. But there was a shaking of heads. Old Thady was known to have a streak of wildness in his character, and anyway such procedure didn't seem quite proper. Hour after hour they sat in silence smoking their pipes, each man turning over in his mind the events of the preceding week in as far as he could remember them. Everyone had a distinct recollection of having been at a funeral, and several remembered the ass cart going down the road with two men sitting on the coffin. It was felt that Pat's Tommy had been under close observation all the time, and it was not understood how he had managed to get out.

During the following day Pat's Tommy passed several of his acquaintances on the road and bade them the time of day. He even dropped in at one man's cottage and borrowed a pitchfork without the owner's permission. An hour after sunset Old Thady found him in the kitchen helping himself liberally to Thady's poteen. Thady saw no reason for remaining, but retreated through the back door as soon as courtesy permitted. When Pat's Tommy took to joining the men at the crossroads at night, sitting there smoking his pipe without a word, a profound gloom settled on the community. Cloonaturk was never much given to conversation, but it was at the meeting-place at the crossroads that a man was afforded an opportunity of making a remark about the weather or about the government, if he felt it incumbent upon him to do so. Now, nobody ventured to say anything; for naturally enough no one wanted to lay himself open to the possibility of contradiction by a corpse. It was felt that it would be unlucky; so the Cloonaturk men smoked in silence, tapped out their pipes one by one, bade Pat's Tommy good night and trudged home.

It's strange how news travels. A week later a newspaperman from one of the Dublin newspapers arrived at the police station. He wore a shabby waterproof coat and an old battered hat, and his face was bright with whiskey.

'Where's Cloonaturk?' he asked.

The Sergeant scowled at him.

'It's on the coast about twelve miles to the west.'

'I hear that a dead man has come back and is walking round Cloonaturk. Did you hear the story?'

'Of course I heard it.'

'Is it true?' asked the newspaperman.

'How do I know whether it's true? I wouldn't be surprised at anything that might happen in that place.'

'Why are you so violent about it?'

The Sergeant made a mighty effort at self-control.

'Listen here,' he said. 'I like a romantic story as well as anyone. In fact, I read them to the children. But I like to find my romance between the covers of a book. I have every reason to be indignant when it manifests itself in a part of my sub-district.'

'So you believe it's true?'

'Get to hell out of this,' roared the Sergeant.

The newspaperman went out and hired a car. Then he bought himself a half-pint bottle of whisky, as he thought he'd need it before he faced the ghost. When he arrived at Cloonaturk and convinced the inhabitants that he wasn't an official, they became quite friendly. The entire population accompanied him down the road in the failing evening light and pointed out to him Pat's Tommy climbing over a stile, Pat's Tommy milking a goat and Pat's Tommy entering the door of his cottage. The newspaperman couldn't see anything, but he was conscious of the approach of night and of the cold, damp wind blowing across the grey Atlantic. He shuddered, drank the whisky, and decided to postpone closer investigation until the daylight. He spent the night in Old Thady's cottage drinking Thady's poteen. On the following day he was able to see all that was pointed out to him, and even more.

The newspaperman was a conscientious reporter and, however drunk he was, he never forgot his obligations to his paper. He got into the hired car and drove five miles to the church to inspect the Register of Deaths. He avoided an accident more by instinct than by good driving, for his view of the road was much impeded by Pat's Tommy, who accompanied him sitting astride the bonnet of the car. At the church he examined the entry in the register, and back in the town he interviewed the coroner and the doctor. Then he telephoned the story to his newspaper in Dublin.

His editor was sceptical. 'I'll hold the story for a few days,' he said. 'And for God's sake, try to sober up.'

'I'm not drunk,' squealed the reporter indignantly.

'Were you ever any other way?' growled the editor.

The newspaperman returned to Cloonaturk, but he only lasted three days. He found the pace too hot. He never quite got used to Pat's Tommy buttonholing him on the road and engaging him in abstruse political argument. He was gone from Cloonaturk one morning and was subsequently heard of in various midland towns where he was in process of drinking himself sober in the course of his return to Dublin. When he reported to his office a week later and his editor saw the state he was in, angry words were spoken. But it wasn't until he threw open the door to show Pat's Tommy sitting on the stairs, that his editor gave him the sack, and tearing the Report, flung it in the wastepaper basket.

So the outside world ceased to take an interest in Cloonaturk, and it was left to the inhabitants to employ their own resources in dealing with the phenomenon. They drank more deeply so as to assist thought. To their alarm, Pat's Tommy, who had always been a quiet man, began to manifest every evidence of a nasty and interfering disposition. It became usual for him to enter a house uninvited just as a man was pouring himself a drink, and knock the bottle out of his hand. He took Long Joe by the throat one night and tried to throw him into the river. Worst of all, he began to hide each house's store of liquor, so that it became commonplace for a man to be compelled to spend half the evening in a desperate search, crawling round the floor of his cottage on his hands and knees with his tongue hanging out. This final outrage convinced the inhabitants that action of a revolutionary nature was called for.

'I'll see the priest,' announced Old Thady to the haggard inhabitants clustered beneath the bank at the crossroads.

'I'll go with you,' volunteered Long Joe, 'because if something isn't done soon, there'll be nothing for it but for the whole of us to emigrate to America.'

'You're right, Long Joe,' said Old Thady, 'and I for one don't want to end my days driving a streetcar in New York.'

In the parlour of the Presbytery, Father Murphy sat back in his armchair and gazed sternly at the two men who stood in the centre of his carpet firmly clutching their battered top hats, which they had refused to surrender to his housekeeper. There were grim lines about the priest's mouth as he listened to their halting tale. When the story had faded away to its miserable conclusion, he breathed fiercely through his nostrils.

'Kneel down, the two of you,' he commanded.

Old Thady and Long Joe looked at one another and then slowly went down on their knees on the hearthrug. They watched anxiously as the priest took out a prayerbook, a pen, and two printed forms.

'I'm going to administer the Pledge against the Consumption of Alcoholic Liquors,' he declared, 'and shall both of you affix your names to the Solemn Declaration.'

A startled look came to the face of each delinquent and remained there.

'Is there no other way you can exorcise Pat's Tommy, Father?' enquired Old Thady brokenly.

'None,' replied the priest severely. 'I'll visit Cloonaturk on Sunday and administer the Pledge to every man in the townland.'

There was a moment's silence; then Old Thady and Long Joe exchanged a mournful glance and rose awkwardly to their feet.

'We're sorry to have troubled you, Father,' said Old Thady abjectly, 'but we'd rather put up with Pat's Tommy. Maybe in time we'll get used to him.'

The priest only remained to watch through the window the two long-coated figures walking slowly across the gravel from his door; then he put on his outdoor clothes himself and went to the back of the house to take out his car.

The Sergeant rose respectfully to his feet as Father Murphy strode into the police station.

'I don't know what the authorities are doing,' said the priest angrily. 'The whole of Cloonaturk is poisoned body and soul.'

'Ah, sure that place—' began the Sergeant.

'I'm not going to waste time talking to you,' snapped the priest. 'Give me that telephone, and tell me the number of the Superintendent of the Area.'

A week later two hundred police, drawn from the neighbouring towns and villages, converged on Cloonaturk from all sides. A cordon was flung around the townland, and four lorryloads of spades were unloaded. The community was in too wretched a condition to hide anything or to try to deceive anyone. The townland was mapped out in square yards, and digging operations commenced. The inhabitants watched from the doors of their cottages in profound melancholy as still after still was unearthed.

'We made one mistake,' said Old Thady. 'I've heard that in other parts of the world a bull is always kept in the neighbourhood of a still, and released when them fellows in uniform get too near.'

'I've heard that too,' replied Long Joe, 'and a field where a still is kept, should always have a barbed wire fence around it. I've been told,' he added gloomily, 'that it's the greatest fun in the world when the bull is let out, to see them police leaving half their pants behind on the top of a barbed wire fence.'

'Are you going to prosecute, sir?' the Sergeant asked the

Superintendent as the stills were being loaded onto the lorries.

'No,' answered the Superintendent gruffly. 'It would cause too much of a scandal. The least said about the affair the better.'

Pat's Tommy was only seen spasmodically during the succeeding week, as the sense of their grievous loss had a sobering effect on the community. Each time that he manifested himself, he was paler and more shadowy. Ten days later he was seen for the last time. In that unearthly hour between twilight and nightfall Long Joe came on him sitting on the bridge lighting his pipe; but even before the pipe was well drawn, he had faded into nothingness, and Long Joe, gazing where he had been, could see nothing but the stream below the bridge spreading out across the sand as it lost itself in the grey Atlantic breakers.

Age Cannot Wither

SHE HAD haunted the harbour for a week, the little old woman with the black shawl over her head, moving with quick steps here and there along the grass-grown quays questioning the loungers on the wall and the out-of-work dockers who sat all day spitting into the water. Day after day she had repeated the same question, her sharp face poking itself out from the cowl of her shawl: 'When do youse expect the ship from Valparaiso?'

The dockers answered her kindly: 'You can never tell with these old-fashioned sailing ships. Any day now.'

No disappointment showed on her grey wrinkled face. She would push the wisp of white hair back from her forehead with a shaking hand, while her sparrowlike eyes darted a quick look across the bay. Then she would turn and hurry away, back up the hill into the town.

'Who the hell is she anyway?' asked one of the quayside loungers. 'I know the phiz of her well. She's always standing at the door of one of the houses in Saint Teresa's Terrace.'

'Ay, she has a Council cottage there. The name is Mrs. Mullarkey. A decent, poor old soul. The husband died on her about fifteen years back.'

'What's she worryin' about the nitrate ship for? Has she someone on board?'

'Tom Hood's on board. A son of a cousin of hers, I think. I don't know what she's so anxious about. These old ones get queer.'

Now that she was old, she no longer slept soundly at night. She would drowse for an hour on her mattress and then lie awake staring upwards at the ceiling, her fingers gripping the ragged counterpane and her old mind busy with vague memories and calculations. Then she would doze and slumber fitfully, to start suddenly wide awake and find her few sticks of furniture visible in the indifferent morning light that filtered in through the torn lace curtains. This last week she slept even less easily, but lay awake hour after hour, listening to the western wind pushing at the tumbledown roofs of the town, rattling casements and whimpering through the streets, while from the bay below came the low, muffled pounding of the Atlantic. She lay still and listened, from time to time smiling to herself and sucking at her few blackened teeth.

Despite all her vigilance she missed the arrival of the ship. She was at the post office on Friday, drawing the old age pension, when a mass of brown sail rounded the headland and came regally across the bay. She was going from one huckster's shop to another carefully picking her week's groceries, while the knot of men on the pier crowded round the stevedore, pushing and shoving, and begging to be taken on for the unloading. She had loitered for an hour in Victoria Lane gossiping and joking with old cronies, so that when she reached St. Teresa's Terrace with her purchases clutched tightly in a fold of her shawl, she was startled to see the ship at the quayside with all its sail furled. She broke into an absurd, little run, and only delayed in her cottage long enough to place the groceries on the dresser, before making her way hurriedly downhill to the harbour.

The sailors were already coming from the ship, walking up the harbour road towards the public house. She screwed up her eyes as she hurried towards them, trying to identify at a distance the man for whom she was looking. At last she saw him walking between two of his mates, stalwart, young, blue-jersied men like himself. She stopped when she sighted him, and when the three men came abreast of where she stood, she cried out a greeting and stepped into the roadway to intercept him. He nodded curtly to her, but did not pause in his stride.

'Have you nothing for me, Tom Hood? Remember what you promised me.'

Tom Hood made no answer, but continued on his way between his two companions. With the humility of the aged she trailed along a couple of paces behind him, her head bowed, intent on not being left behind. She broke into a little run now and then when the steady, dogged stride of the young men threatened to increase the distance between them. She was quite out-of-breath when they reached the public house. His two companions bent their heads and entered the low doorway, but Tom Hood turned to face her. She was breathing heavily.

'You haven't forgot your promise, Tom?' she wheedled. The young man fumbled clumsily in his trouser pocket and at last brought out a battered, square tobacco tin.

'Here they are,' he said gruffly, 'and be careful of them. They're as fierce as I said.'

The old woman clutched at the box, turned it over in her hand and hid it quickly in the recesses of her shawl.

'The blessings of God on you, Tom. Sure, I knew I could rely on you not to forget.'

'Remember,' there was a note of menace in his voice, 'not a word to anyone that it was from me you got them.'

'I promise, Tom, I promise.'

The young man turned on his heel without another word and entered the doorway of the tavern. Only when she was back in her room did the old woman venture to lift the lid of the tin box. She opened it ever so carefully, only the tiniest crack. She held the box close to her eyes and tried to peer within. From the box came the sound of irritated buzzing.

Cautiously she closed it again, and a slow, delighted leer crept across her face.

*   *   *

In his office on the first floor of Moymell Town Hall, Stanislaus MacVeale sat very upright at his desk neatly affixing his signature to the bundle of letters fresh from the typist. The telephone on his desk rang. He placed his fountain pen carefully on the inkstand and lifted the receiver with a short, precise motion.

'MacVeale, Sanitary Officer, speaking.'

'This is Boyce.'

'Who?'

'Boyce, foreman of the Decontamination Squad.'

'Oh, Boyce. What is it? Anything wrong?'

'It's that case of Mrs. Mullarkey of St. Teresa's Terrace, which was reported this morning. I think you ought to come over and see for yourself, sir.'

'Is the bedding infested, as she said?'

'Something shocking. In all my born days I never encountered such bugs. It's an education even to see them. You'll be real interested, sir.'

'Why should I be interested?' snapped the Sanitary Officer. 'It's only a case of burning the bedding. I'll authorise the usual free issue of new mattress and blankets. Better have the infected stuff carried out and burnt at once. There's no need for me to be there: you know what to do.'

There was a moment's silence at the other end of the line. Then Boyce spoke again in a voice that seemed small and apologetic.

'I'd rather you'd come over, sir. The men are — — eh, disinclined to go ahead.'

'What! Do you mean to say that they refuse to obey your orders?'

71

'The men are all right,' came Boyce's voice. 'They'll do anything within reason. But I'm short-handed. I've only Old Dominic left. John Mortimer was badly bitten about the wrist, and in about three minutes he was taken sudden with what you might call involuntary twitchings of the hands and arms. I had to send the other man out with him to help him across to the hospital.'

'Have you been drinking, Boyce?'

'Honest to God, sir, not a drop since Easter. You wouldn't say that if you saw poor John Mortimer being assisted along St. Teresa's Terrace with every limb jerking as if he was on a griddle, and a crowd of people walking alongside following his motions with the greatest interest.'

'Look here, Boyce,' said the Sanitary Officer grimly, 'I don't want any of that romancing.' He hesitated for a moment. 'All right,' he said gruffly, 'I'll be over myself.'

He replaced the receiver and rose sharply to his feet. He took his well-brushed overcoat from the back of the door, and as he fastened the belt, the nickname which the town had applied to him, half in malice and half in contempt, came into his mind—'Efficiency MacVeale'. He smiled slightly as he opened the door, and proceeded to make his way down the stairs to his car.

When he drew up in St. Teresa's Terrace he found a small crowd on the pavement outside Mrs. Mullarkey's door. They made way for him respectfully, and he entered the cottage. An old woman was sitting on a kitchen chair in the middle of the floor moaning to herself and wringing her hands. The two surviving members of the Decontamination Squad stood awkwardly by the door, Boyce stolid but rather shame-faced, and Dominic, a little, old man, wearing a hard hat and an overcoat so very much too big for him that it concealed his hands, and nearly reaching to the floor, gave him the appearance of one of those legless, wooden figures from a child's Noah's Ark. Dominic had been in the Council's employment well-nigh fifty years, and should have been retired long ago, but no one had the heart to hint to him that he was growing old, so he was being constantly passed from one department to another. His last assignment had been to the Town Fire Brigade, but the captain had declared forcibly that the only work he'd be any good for, would be sitting on the hose to stop the leaks; so when the new Sanitary Officer had formed the Decontamination Squad, Old Dominic had been immediately passed on to him as a suitable recruit.

When he saw Mr. MacVeale, Dominic immediately came to attention and flapped one of his sleeves up to the bent brim of his hat in a semi-military salute.

Ignoring him, the Sanitary Officer addressed himself to Boyce: 'What in hell's name is going on here?'

'I'm glad to see you, sir,' said the foreman with evident relief. 'If you'll be so good as to look at this mattress and bedding —— '

Mr. MacVeale poked cautiously at the ragged bedclothes.

'I wouldn't do that, sir,' put in Dominic hastily. 'It's no use makin' em' cross.'

'That's how Mortimer got bitten,' added Boyce respectfully.

'Bitten!' ejaculated Dominic hoarsely. 'They caught him by the wrist and tried to pull him under the blankets.'

'Don't be absurd,' snapped the Sanitary Officer.

'I beg pardon,' said Dominic meekly, 'but I seen them with these two eyes. I wouldn't put anythin' past them fellows. Real fierce-looking characters.'

The Sanitary Officer breathed impatiently. 'What do they look like?'

'Not like the usual ones at all,' replied the foreman. 'Ordinary bugs are rusty red with traces of yellow. These ones are tawny and of exceptional girth.'

73

'As big as elephants,' put in Dominic, 'so help me God. If you put your ear down near the bed, sir, you can hear them ripping away at the cloth and growling at one another.'

Mr. MacVeale turned his back pointedly and addressed himself to Boyce.

'Better drag out the lot and burn it. If you don't want to handle it, take the grappling irons from the back of the Town Hall.'

He turned to the old woman in the chair. 'I'm very sorry, madam, but I have that power under the Council's by-laws. These insects multiply so rapidly that one must act with the utmost despatch. To compensate you for your loss, the Council will issue you with a new mattress and bedding. In fact, you will gain by the exchange, so don't take it too much to heart.'

'It's terrible what the poor has to suffer,' sighed Mrs. Mullarkey between her tears, 'but I thank you humbly all the same, sir.'

'It's a lucky thing for you, ma'am,' said Dominic, 'that them lads haven't got into the walls and behind the plaster. We'd have had to pull the house down.'

'God looks after the poor,' sighed the old woman.

'By the way, Boyce,' said the Sanitary Officer turning at the door, 'try to get me a specimen. I'd like to see it, and maybe send it for identification.'

Late that evening envious neighbours crowded into Mrs. Mullarkey's room to admire her new tick mattress and the army blankets which she displayed with conscious pride. When she retired at last to rest, it was with the air of a queen. She snuggled into the blankets breathing in their sensuous cleanliness, and passed at last into a dreamless slumber with a smirk on her crinkled face.

*   *   *

A fortnight later two clerks sitting at their desks in the Town Hall, bent their heads and pretended to be assiduously at work as the door opened and the Sanitary Officer came in with a sheet of paper in his hand. He looked careworn.

'They've identified it at last. I have a report from the Zoological Department in Dublin. It's a wingless Chilean bug, hitherto unknown in this country. I've been doing a bit of hard thinking. It may have come in with that nitrate ship.'

One of the clerks made a sympathetic sound. 'I've ordered another hundred army blankets and mattresses as you said, sir.'

'I don't know how I'll face the County Manager,' sighed Mr. MacVeale. 'This will mean another threepence on the rates.'

'And it's still spreading,' added the clerk. 'Every Council house in St. Teresa's Terrace is infested, and it's creeping up the neighbouring lanes.'

For a moment the Sanitary Officer looked grey and old. He did not reply, but went back to his room and seated himself at his desk. He sat for a long time thinking of the scenes he had witnessed during the past two weeks, the Council workmen armed with blowlamps manfully fighting the intruders up and down the stairs of the new Council houses.

'The bloody old fool,' grinned the elder of the two clerks as he resumed his seat. ' "Efficiency MacVeale" indeed! And half the town knows that the old dame is hiring out the bugs at so much a time.'

His companion sniggered. 'I was told she was in Maguire's reach-me-down shop at the corner of Victoria Lane last night buying herself a fur coat.'

Leo the Lion

Mr. Bullitt watched the last peg being hammered deep into the sandy soil. Then he stepped back and studied the circus tent. He was a squat, broadly-built man with a paunch discreetly modified by a crimson waistcoat plentifully ornamented with silver buttons. A partiality for whiskey had etched a lacework of purple veins in his cheeks and served to accentuate his nose, which stood out in the middle of his face like a door knocker.

The erection of the tent had been a troublesome business, and Mr. Bullitt had several times doubted the wisdom of his decision to pitch it in the sand dunes below the town. The sandy soil did not readily grip the wooden pegs, and again and again the ropes had to be lengthened so as to reach to the nearest tuft of grass and firmer soil; but the proximity of the annual horse races, which were run on the strand, was an important commercial consideration.

Mr. Bullitt stood for a moment preoccupied, his chin sunk on his cravat; then he roused himself and made his way between the welter of caravans and circus paraphernalia until he came to a large cage mounted on wheels.

Three urchins were standing in front of it staring in awe at the lion reclining inside. He was a very bedraggled sort of lion, and though his eyes were half-open, he didn't seem to be thinking of anything in particular.

As Mr. Bullitt came to a halt, the oldest of the urchins was slowly reading aloud the faded inscription which ran in curly letters along the top of the cage: 'Leo the Man-Eating Lion.'

'Gawd!' whispered the smallest boy. 'Isn't he awful?'

76

Mr. Bullitt dug a match from the pocket of his crimson waistcoat and lighted it with a quick stroke on his fingernail. He applied the flame to his cheroot and made a loud, sucking sound. The lion immediately raised a moth-eaten snout, and he and Mr. Bullitt contemplated each other in silence. Leo, however, appeared to see nothing of interest in Mr. Bullitt, and the effort of gazing at his owner seemed to exhaust him: his tawny eyes became glazed, he blinked in a bored fashion, wrinkled up his nose and opened his mouth in a colossal yawn.

'He hasn't got any teeth,' hissed one of the small boys.

'Get to hell out of here!' snapped Mr. Bullitt, making a threatening move in the direction of the youngsters, who immediately broke and scuttled away between the tents. The circus owner turned on his heel and went up the steps into the caravan where Hercule the Lion-tamer was sitting on a stool before the bucket which contained the gruel for Leo's evening meal.

'That animal,' began Mr. Bullitt, 'that animal isn't in a fit state to be seen. Folks are beginning to take notice that he hasn't got any teeth. You should have screwed in his dentures before we came into town.'

Hercule paused in his work and glanced across at the two huge dental plates which hung from a nail on the far wall. They were a masterpiece of the dental surgeon's art.

'Leo is gettin' old,' objected Hercule. 'He don't like having all that furniture in his mouth unnecessarily.'

'You don't have to tell me that he's gettin' old,' snapped Mr. Bullitt. 'He's a bleedin' Methuselah, but that's got nothing to do with it. We've got to keep the public in mind.'

A look of obstinacy settled suddenly on the lion-tamer's face. 'You wouldn't like to have to walk round yourself,' he said, 'with a set of massive things like that clamped between your jaws.'

'He doesn't have to walk round. All he has to do is lie in his cage all day in the lap of luxury, swalleyin' the best of food and drink. He's better off than any of us. Anyway, his personal feelings have nothing to do with the matter. We all have to make sacrifices in the show business.'

'All right,' muttered Hercule.

'Another thing,' said Mr. Bullitt, peering into the bucket. 'We'll have to cut down on his grub. About half that much will do. You can keep the rest for his breakfast.'

Hercule breathed hard through his nostrils. 'How can the unfortunate animal be expected to do himself justice in his act when he's weak with the hunger? We've been cuttin' down on his grub for the past six weeks. First, we deprived him of his bit of meat —— '

'Meat is bad for him at his age. It'll only give him blood pressure. I can't afford to have him dying on my hands, a valuable animal like that. Anyway, it's a question of economics. Some of you fellows seem to think I'm made of money.'

'That's another thing,' said the lion-tamer meaningly. 'The staff is beginning to speculate as to whether they're ever going to be paid again. The clowns in particular is talking mighty nasty.'

Mr. Bullitt stared at him for a moment, as if undecided whether or not to lose his temper. Then he removed the damp and shapeless cheroot from his mouth. 'Come on out and have a drink. They've set up a bar on the strand.'

From the edge of the sand dunes the whole fawn-coloured expanse of beach lay stretched before them, mile after mile of unbroken sand. They made their way toward the straggling crowd of some three or four hundred people which had congregated in the corner of the strand where the races were being held. Yokels stood about with their hands in their pockets staring at nothing or wandered aimlessly about.

The town's corner-boys were clustered in the neighbour-hood of the bookmakers' pitch, where four portly individuals in check suits and hard gray hats were shouting the odds for the last race. Near by, half a dozen planks had been laid across upright barrels and crowned with a thin railing.

This was the judges' stand, and the three judges seemed to have brought their families and all their friends along with them. The women and girls did not mingle with the men, but sat in little groups at the edge of the sand dunes drinking lemonade and eating sweets from paper bags.

'It's a shabby affair,' said the lion-tamer morosely.

'These small-town races always are,' replied Mr. Bullitt.

Together they made their way to the refreshment tent. Their entry caused a stir of interest. As they pushed through the crowd toward the plank resting on two empty tea-chests, which served as counter, room was made for them in the place of honour beside the police sergeant, a huge man whose mottled face was half submerged in a pint tumbler.

'Good evening, gentlemen,' said Mr. Bullitt, drawing a crumpled note from the pocket of his scarlet waistcoat and tossing it carelessly on the counter. There was a chorus of 'Good evening, sir,' from the circle of drinkers.

'You're the gentleman that runs the circus?' the sergeant asked.

'Yes, I'm Mr. Bullitt.'

'I see that you have a whole menagerie of animals advertised. Ever since I was a child I've had a great liking for the animals you meet in a circus.'

Mr. Bullitt coughed and looked at the floor. 'We've had a heavy loss lately. The buffalo died on us. The posters were already printed, and I haven't had time to have them altered.'

'That's too bad,' said the sergeant sympathetically.

'Was that long ago?' inquired a foxy man with a red scarf, who stood leaning on the counter beyond the sergeant.

Mr. Bullitt raised his eyes and looked at the stranger suspiciously. The words seemed to have been too softly spoken to be without some ulterior meaning. The man with the red scarf was a thin, auburn-haired fellow with a suggestion of a smile hovering permanently in the neighbourhood of his mouth.

'About four years ago,' replied Mr. Bullitt brusquely and turned again to the sergeant. 'It's a wonder,' he said in a bantering tone, 'that the police don't keep a better eye on the young ruffians of a town and not have them murdering valuable animals.'

The sergeant grinned: 'The poor police. People expect them to be everywhere. The Race Committee has been at me all week to have the strand patrolled so as to keep the young monkeys from moving the flags that mark the course.'

A small sportily-dressed gentleman who had been listening intently, could contain himself no longer. 'These races are nothing but a hoax,' he burst out savagely. 'The judges are slipping down from the stand and betting money on the horses themselves. I've seen them doing it myself. It's a scandal.'

The sergeant emitted a great shout of laughter. He turned his sweating face to Mr. Bullitt. 'Have you any animals at all in that circus of yours, or is it a hoax too?'

Mr. Bullitt stiffened. 'We have a man-eating lion, a most valuable animal. I wouldn't part with that animal for five hundred pounds.'

'Did he ever eat anyone yet?' inquired the foxy man with the red scarf.

Mr. Bullitt did not deign to reply. Instead, he turned to the sergeant. 'Who's your companion?' he inquired coldly.

'Him? Do you not know him? I thought that rogue was known throughout the length and breadth of the land. He's Larry Hamill, the slipperiest poacher in the whole country.

I've been trying to catch him for the past fifteen years and I haven't succeeded yet.'

From long experience on the road, Mr. Bullitt knew the expediency of being on good terms with the representatives of the law, so he permitted himself a tight smile, but it faded as he caught sight of the quizzical mockery in Larry Hamill's face.

'Tell us about the last man your lion killed.'

Mr. Bullitt stared disdainfully at the ragged poacher, but he could think of nothing crushing to say. He turned and looked at Hercule for assistance, but the lion-tamer merely dropped his eyes and looked into his empty glass.

'Another two whiskies,' snapped Mr. Bullitt.

When their glasses had been refilled, and Mr. Bullitt had slowly and thoughtfully placed a couple of coins on the counter, he turned and threw a contemptuous glance at the foxy-headed poacher. Then he cleared his throat importantly and addressed himself to the whole circle of listeners.

'The thing to remember about wild beasts is that, though they may be trained, they can never in fact be tamed. Isn't that so, Hercule?'

The lion-tamer nodded bleakly.

The circus owner fixed his eyes haughtily on the poacher's red scarf. 'You will understand that it is impossible for me openly to admit that Leo has taken human life. I would be cutting my own throat if I made such an admission, for the authorities would insist that he be destroyed. Isn't that so, Sergeant?'

The sergeant nodded in confirmation.

'In the interest of the show business my lips are sealed, but I can assure you that no more bloody-minded beast has ever walked the jungle. I doubt if his like has ever been seen for cold ferocity.'

The audience was visibly impressed.

'The last lion-tamer I had was so foolish as once to turn his back on Leo. He has regretted it every since.'

'What happened?' inquired the sergeant in a small voice.

'With one blow of his paw,' said Mr. Bullitt dramatically, 'Leo swept the buttock off him. Never the same man after.'

'It seems to be a dangerous occupation, lion-taming,' commented the sergeant. 'I wouldn't fancy it at all.'

'Dangerous!' echoed Mr. Bullitt. 'The first lion tamer I had—well. I'd prefer not to talk about it.'

He raised his hat reverently, and turning, gulped down his whiskey as if the recollection of the terrible scene were too much for him. A gloom settled on his listeners. They stood silent, their pint tumblers gripped in their fists, staring dejectedly in front of them as if in sorrowful contemplation of the many hazards to which human life is subject. At that moment a man pushed his way through the crowd.

'You'd better come quick, Sergeant. They've chased a welshing bookmaker into the sea, and he refuses to come out without police protection.'

The sergeant buttoned the collar of his tunic and left the tent. Mr. Bullitt, well satisfied with the impression which he had made, signed to Hercule, and they also pushed their way out into the open air. They walked back in silence towards the caravans among the sand dunes.

The circus tent was crowded that night, and the spectators watched breathlessly as Leo was put through his paces. Hercule guided the lion with a long whip from one high stool to another. Leo climbed and sprang as directed, growling forlornly as he felt the twinges of rheumatism. When he sat on the highest stool of all and looked at the distance he would have to climb down again, he raised his muzzle in the air and howled heartbrokenly.

The sergeant in the front row wiped the sweat from his forehead and thought of the fate of Hercule's predecessors.

The lion-tamer kept Leo on the move, tipping and prodding him with the long whip, because there was a danger that if Leo was left for a few minutes sitting in the one place, he would fall asleep.

At length the lion was guided down again, growling and complaining, to the floor of the cage, and Mr. Bullitt, stalking to the centre of the arena, announced in ringing tones the high spot of the evening—the intrepid Hercule would now place his head in the lion's mouth. A shudder of expectancy rippled through the audience, there was a roll of drums, and a green spotlight picked out Leo as he wearily opened his mouth and displayed his terrible fangs.

Hercule laid aside the whip and approached cautiously. He placed his two hands on Leo's corrugated cheeks, and unnoticed by the audience, slipped the usual block of wood between the lion's back teeth, just in case Leo should grow tired of holding his mouth open and close it without giving due warning. Then the intrepid Hercule carefully introduced his head between Leo's gigantic dentures.

Women screamed and buried their faces on the shoulders of their escorts, while the men, with white faces, stared fascinated at the terrible spectacle. Slowly Hercule withdrew his head, there was another roll of drums, and he stood bowing in the centre of the ring amid a thunder of applause.

When the lights in the great tent had been extinguished, and a couple of cowboys were treading their way between the caravans essaying the impossible task of hunting the children of the town away from the circus ground, Leo ambled slowly across his cage and peered into the bucket which contained his supper.

At first he could scarcely believe his eyes. He stared incredulously but there was no mistake—the bucket was only half-full. He looked to left and right, and then, opening his jaws, emitted an indignant roar. It was a hollow, reverberating roar, which seemed to come from the depths of his stomach. Two small boys who had been fiddling with the catch on the door of the cage, immediately sprang to the ground and raced off into the darkness.

Leo did not even bother to glance after them. He knew that the bars of the cage were there to protect him from human beings, and that as long as the bars were intact, he was safe; so he paid no attention to noises outside. Anyway, his mind was too taken up with his wrongs. He kept his eyes fixed on his meagre supper, growling at the bucket as he gradually backed away from it until his hindquarters came in contact with the door.

To his astonishment he felt the door open behind him. He turned his head and studied this extraordinary phenomenon, slowly coming to a realization of the infinite possibilities which were opening before him. Normally he would never have thought of exchanging the safety of his cage for the unknown dangers of the outside world, but his mood at the moment was one of extreme exasperation.

If they weren't going to give him his customary measure of food, be damned but he'd go and get it for himself. He paused for a moment only at the open door, then bounded softly to the ground. He stood for a short while sniffing the air to left and right, his tail lashing gently; then he padded off cautiously into the darkness.

Early the following morning Hercule burst into Mr. Bullitt's caravan with the news of the calamity. The circus magnate sat up in his bunk in his nightshirt and upraided the lion-tamer.

'He must be got back at once or it's the end of us. We're near enough to bankruptcy as it is, without losing our star performer. You hear me: he must be got back!'

The news spread with astonishing rapidity. When the sergeant was informed that Leo the Man-Eating Lion was abroad, he turned white. He fumbled and dropped his keys as he hurried to open the station cupboard to issue revolvers to his men. About midday a furious barking of dogs announced the breakneck arrival of a bread truck in the town. The driver sprang from the truck and shouted his news, that three miles out in the country he had seen a telegraph linesman marooned up a pole while Leo lay fast asleep at the base. The linesman had shouted piteously that he had been up the pole for two hours, that he was riddled with cramp and that he expected to fall off any moment.

A volunteer party with scythes and pitchforks crowded into the cars which the police quickly commandeered, and set out for the scene, but on their arrival they found nothing of Leo except some moulted hair. The linesman had to be taken from the telegraph pole by ladder. He was quite incapable of giving an articulate account of the affair and had to be assisted to walk by two men holding him under the armpits. He was conveyed back to the town and put to bed in the County Hospital.

By early afternoon, all the schoolmasters in the neighbourhood had got through on the phone to the Department of Education and obtained permission to close their schools.

'What I'm afraid of,' said the lion-tamer, 'is that some of these yahoos of policemen will frighten Leo. A sudden shock at his age might have serious consequences. They're tearing around the countryside on bicycles with revolvers. You can never trust a policeman to act sensible: they're that wild when they get excited, they might even open fire and injure the poor inoffensive animal. Oh, Mr. Bullitt, sir, Leo has been with us a long time now. You'll have to do something to save him. Can't you go to the sergeant and explain that he's the most harmless lion that ever walked on four paws? Honest, boss, that animal is innocent. I don't believe that in all his life he has even had a bad thought.'

85

'Keep your mouth shut. He has been billed for years as an animal of most unexampled ferocity. Do you want to have me prosecuted for fraud? Anyway, if it's made public that he's nothing but a sissy, we might as well take his act out of the show, and where'd we be then? In the bankruptcy court, every man jack of us.'

That evening when it was reported that Leo had been sighted on the railway line some miles outside the town, an engine-driver refused to take his train out of the station. He was backed strongly by the fireman, who insisted that he had seen in the films lions springing unerringly from overhanging trees on to innocent passers-by.

Neither threats of dismissal nor bribes could move the engine-driver. There were too many overhead bridges on the line, he said; he didn't mind for himself, but he had a wife and five children dependent on him. The passengers had to be accommodated for the night in the railway station.

'I don't think I'll be able to sleep,' said the lion-tamer sorrowfully, 'when I think of that poor animal with nowhere to lay his head.'

'I wish I could lay my hands on him,' said Mr. Bullitt savagely. 'He has the whole life of the county paralyzed.'

Mr. Bullitt's temper was not improved by the arrival the following morning of a farmer claiming compensation for the loss of a goat, shot dead during the night by a nervous policeman, whose only excuse was that it had failed to answer his challenge . . .

Some five miles away in a small belt of trees Leo lay, his chin resting dejectedly on his great soft paws. Half an hour before, while sheltering in a ditch beside the road, he had been startled by the sudden appearance of a small boy on a bicycle. The unusual sight had nearly thrown Leo into convulsions. He had flung himself in desperation through the hedge and made off across the fields.

It was the worst thing that he had yet experienced, and his heart was still thumping against his ribs. On the previous day he had ambled along the road until the pads of his paws were sore from the hard macadam, telling himself that sooner or later he would surely come on something to eat. Then he had tried the railway line for a bit, but he had found the sleepers so placed as to render a prolonged walk uncomfortable, and you couldn't trot on them at all.

Now he lay motionless except for a slight twitching of the ears, wishing to Heaven that he was safe back in his cage. He lay there hour after hour until the urge of hunger became so strong that he could not bear to remain still any longer. He reared himself slowly to his feet, moaned plaintively, and started to wander disconsolately across the field.

As he was mooching through a gap, he saw something which brought him to a sudden halt. A few paces from where he stood, a fox terrier puppy was nuzzling a bone. It was a very large bone, far too big for so small a dog: in fact it was nearly as big as itself. When the puppy saw Leo, the eyes nearly popped out of its head. For one moment it gazed incredulously. Then it rolled over on its back, all its paws relaxed in a token of surrender.

But Leo was not taking any chances: he had once been bitten by a furious Sealyham which had managed to worm its way between the bars of his cage, so his approach was wary. When he was near enough, he put out a cautious paw and quickly flicked the bone in his own direction. In a moment he had it between his teeth and was running back the way he had come.

The puppy, apparently of opinion that its last hour had come, was lying on its back with its eyes closed; but when after a reasonable time it was borne in on its mind that nothing was happening to it, it ventured to open its eyes. Observing that the coast was clear, it rolled over onto its paws again, and with its tail between its legs scuttled off as fast as it could in the opposite direction.

Meanwhile Leo, when he adjudged that he was at a safe distance from the fellow-animal which he had wronged, lay down to inspect his loot. It was a toothsome bone with shreds of meat still adhering to it, and his sniffing nose told him that it was packed with marrow inside. He wrapped a paw over the bone so as to keep it steady while he tried to get a grip on it with one side of his jaw.

But the bone was slippery, and the fact that he was wearing false teeth was an additional difficulty. He licked the bone several times, moved over onto one elbow and tried again. With his eyes half-closed and his nose wrinkled almost into a knot, he at last managed to get a firm grip. He exerted all the pressure of which his jaws were capable. There was an ominous crack, and several of his fangs fell out.

In the market square a trembling small boy leaned his bicycle against the town lamppost and related to the horrified crowd, how he had been chased for miles along the road by a lion.

'There's nothing else for it,' said the sergeant, as he picked up the phone. 'I should have done it before. I'm going to call out the military.'

The lion-tamer had been drinking heavily but this was the final blow. He took to his bunk and refused to get up.

'This is the end. They'll riddle the unfortunate animal with bullets.'

'Yes,' said his master bitterly, 'and he's not even insured.'

During the ensuing week, terror possessed the countryside. In outlying farms, behind doors heavily bolted and barred, farmers stood in the centres of their kitchens gripping pitchforks. Upstairs the women of the house tried to quieten the children, while all listened trembling to the soft pad of footsteps in the farmyard outside, the scratching sounds and the inevitable clucking and squawking from the poultry house.

In the morning when the farmer ventured to withdraw the bolts, it was to find that nothing remained but feathers scattered widely in the yard and on the neighbouring road.

'I wouldn't have believed that Leo was capable of it,' said the lion-tamer. 'I don't know what sort of government we have in this country. They can't even catch a wayward lion, who's probably only too anxious to give himself up if he was certain he could do it with safety.'

The authorities in fact were doing their best. A military cordon had been flung around the area, and six sharpshooters were on hand, but while there was a certain amount of banging at night which gave the local people confidence, the only casualties so far had been among livestock.

On the following Saturday evening, Hercule, his face radiant, burst into Mr. Bullitt's caravan.

'Leo has been vindicated!'

Mr. Bullitt sprang from his bunk. 'Have they captured him?'

'No, but his character has been cleared. Last night a farmer named Murphy saw that thieving poacher, Larry Hamill, creeping out of his yard with a sackful of dead hens. The poacher stood in the yard as bold as you please scattering feathers up in the air and in all directions, so as to put the blame on the unfortunate lion. Old Murphy peppered him with a shotgun from the window.'

'That villainous twister! I knew he was no good. The dirty double-crosser! Have they arrested him?'

'No, he's in the County Hospital with the doctors digging the shot out of him with knives. They've arrested Old Murphy and charged him with attempted murder.'

'They can't go on with it. There'll be a revolution in the neighbourhood.'

89

'That's the authorities' lookout. Maybe now that Leo has been proven innocent, the government will call off its gunmen, and we can all get a little sleep.'

The disclosure of the poacher's perfidy was followed by a revulsion of popular feeling in favour of the maligned Leo. It was realised that there was not a tittle of evidence that the lion had done any harm to man or beast; moreover, as he had not been seen for a week, the belief began to grow that he was either deceased or that he had moved out of the neighbourhood altogether.

The local people began to clamour for the withdrawal of the military sharpshooters, who were felt to be a greater danger than the lion. They became confirmed in this belief when one of the sharpshooters shot part of the roof off a poor man's cottage with a tommy-gun one night, leaving the startled tenant and his wife exposed to the stars.

The military were withdrawn, and after a couple of nights undisturbed by random rifle fire, Leo ventured to put his head out of the boghole where he had gone to ground. He was very scraggy and emaciated. His bones were nearly protruding through his hide like the ribs of a broken umbrella.

There was no moon overhead, and no one knew how he found his way back to the circus. Hunger may have sharpened his homing instinct, for he had subsisted for a week on an inadequate vegetable diet, mostly water-cress and nettles. The lion-tamer had hopefully left the door of the cage open, and one morning he was rewarded.

Leo was found squatting on his haunches inside, looking rather sheepish, his paws tar-stained, and his mane full of pieces of brier and bristling with burrs. He was a very sorry-looking lion, but he purred deep down in his throat and rubbed his scarred muzzle against Hercule as the lion-tamer flung his arms round his neck. And Leo noted with satisfaction that, excited as the lion-tamer was, he did not neglect to test every bar of the cage and lock and padlock the door before running to prepare a bumper meal and announce the return of the prodigal.

The Men Who Could Outstare Cobras

No WONDER people stared at Leopardo as he hurried along the pavement. He looked too sedate a man to be walking at such an absurd pace, threading his way in and out among the crowds and even bumping into carelessly-ambling pedestrians, as if he had not seen them. From time to time the passers-by paused and stared after him. His general appearance, the black overcoat of perfect cut and the dove-coloured spats, marked him out as a person of some distinction; there was a dignity in his bearing and a pride in his stern, sombre face which made his nervous haste seem almost indecent. A few recognised him; and an indignant pedestrian with whom he had collided, gripped his companion by the arm and hissed: 'That's Leopardo. Did you see him? Leopardo The World's Greatest Hypnotist.'

Leopardo hurried on his way, the corner of his mouth jerking nervously. He knew that he was attracting attention; but such was his state of mind that he was unable to slacken his pace. Behind the grim, drawn lines of his face his brain was in turmoil: 'I'm giving myself away. Everybody recognises me. I should have taken a taxi from the station. I should have known that they'd all recognise me, with the headlines and my picture in all the papers. Besides, I'm known. In the show business you become known. I'm making a pitiful spectacle of myself, a pitiful spectacle. I', and his mouth stirred contemptuously, 'I, with the strongest will of any man alive!' He emitted a short, bitter laugh; then conscious at once of what he had done, he almost reddened with shame. He closed his eyes for a moment as he walked, lest he should see in the faces of the passers-by that they had heard him. 'Keep your head,' he kept repeating to himself, 'keep your head. People don't recognise you. You're attracting attention unnecessarily.' And by an effort of will, and it seemed to him the hardest thing he had ever done in his life, he slackened his pace until his walk was normal.

Although he was otherwise faultlessly dressed, the dirt of many days had accumulated on his shoes and trouser-ends. He had sat for seven hours in a railway carriage, travelling since early morning all the way from Moymell, where he had at last completed the task which he had set himself. The necessity of finishing the work had sustained him through those ten terrible days and those ten sleepless nights, days and nights in which he had travelled from town to town correcting the wrong he had done. Cold, iron determination had brought him through, had enabled him to face the unfriendly crowds milling back and forward in the streets of those small towns, and face the gnawing fear of prosecution which had been with him all the time: the police, prosecution and a prison sentence. When it was all over, the iron will had slipped . . . his iron will which had never failed him before . . . had slipped . . . over the edge and into deep water. He had sat hour after hour crumpled in the corner of the railway carriage, toying and fidgeting with a newspaper until he had torn it all to pieces. He had almost come to believe that the railway journey would never end. The narrow walls and ceiling of the carriage had pressed too closely in upon him, bringing to consciousness images of a prison cell or a padded den in the madhouse. It was in the carriage that he had finally made up his mind. Of all the people he knew, he hated most to have to ask assistance of that one man to whose house he was now hurrying, but there was nothing else for it; so, when the train had slid into Central Station and he had escaped from the carriage, he made straight for a telephone.

The careful voice of the male receptionist at the other end had been at first deprecatory; it was quite impossible to see the Professor without a prior appointment . . . the appointment book was very full . . . perhaps in ten days' time; but when the receptionist had heard the famous name Leopardo, he had excused himself and gone to enquire . . . certainly, the Professor would cancel two other appointments that afternoon and would be pleased to see Mr. Leopardo at four o'clock. And so The World's Greatest Hypnotist had started to walk through the streets towards Middleton Square. He had not taken a taxi; he had three-quarters of an hour to spare, and after the confinement of the railway carriage, he craved physical exercise and the feeling of moving through the free air again.

As he turned the corner into Middleton Square, he made a mighty effort and pulled himself together. There was something in the peace of the eighteenth-century square which helped him . . . the deserted pathways, the cliff-like line of rusty brick mansions each wearing the calm dignity of a more leisurely age, the ornate doorways and the rows of windows looking across with graceful indifference at the massed greenery of the trees, faded and dull and powdered with the dust of gentility. Leopardo walked slowly along the empty pavement until he came to Number 308. There he paused and read the inscription on the brass plate: 'Professor Ampersand, Master Hypnotist'. He turned, resolutely mounted the nine steps, and pressed the bell.

He was reflecting sourly on the irony of the situation, that he, The World's Greatest Hypnotist, should be driven to seek the assistance of a charlatan like Ampersand, when the door before him swung back noiselessly and a grave personage in a dark suit bowed to him and suavely invited him to enter. He stepped into the ornate hall, and the receptionist deftly conducted him to a waiting-room, where

94

he expressed his regrets that it would unfortunately be necessary to keep Mr. Leopardo waiting for a short time as Professor Ampersand could not at the moment be disturbed, being engaged in conducting a rather difficult patient out of a hypnotic slumber. Leopardo nodded curtly and fell to studying the room. There was no doubt about it that Ampersand seemed to be doing very well for himself; expensive magazines lay scattered carelessly on the broad mahogany table, all the furnishings were rich, the carpet was of the thickest turkey. On the mantelpiece there stood a large gilt clock surmounted by an angel blowing a trumpet, 'the gift of his grateful patient, Alderman Spratt, to Professor Samuel Ampersand' On the far wall there hung an early nineteenth-century print of the great Mesmer himself leaning forward in an attitude of great resolution as with his two hands he made frantic passes before the face of a rather startled-looking patient who was represented sitting bolt upright in bed wearing a nightcap of the period. Through the folding doors Leopardo could hear the stertorous breathing and grunting of the patient in the neighbouring room while all the time the Professor's incantatory murmuring rose and fell. It was as if there was a swarm of bees in the neighbourhood, and Leopardo listened with professional interest until a sudden crash announced that the wrestling of wills was over. 'That'll go down in the bill,' he muttered grimly and took his stand at the window to watch the patient's departure. She emerged a few minutes later, an oversized woman in a fur coat, assisted down the steps to the waiting motor-car by the receptionist and a dapperly-uniformed chauffeur.

As Leopardo turned from the window, the door was flung open, and Professor Ampersand advanced with his hands outstretched. Both were conscious of the insincerity of the greeting, and Leopardo unsmilingly held out a single cold hand.

95

'It must be thirty years, thirty long years since we met,' breezed the Professor. 'Come into my consulting room. It's more comfortable than here.'

In the neighbouring room, the receptionist was gathering up the remains of a chair.

'That'll do, Carruthers. Put it anywhere. You may go now. I shan't require you till the morning.'

When the discreet Carruthers had closed the door behind him, Professor Ampersand pulled an armchair forward into a position facing the light and waved his visitor into it. He bustled about procuring cigars and ash-trays; then he disposed his own huge bulk in another armchair filling it completely. As they removed the bands from their cigars the two old friends eyed each other curiously. In appearance they were in remarkable contrast, the lean, sallow Leopardo, grim and ascetic, and Professor Samuel Ampersand with prosperity written right across his ample waistcoat, for Ampersand had grown stout, though his fat did not hide the determined line of his jaw which jutted out from his face like a paving block. 'Rather pre-1914,' thought Leopardo as he noted the pomaded hair plastered down on the Professor's skull, and the huge black moustaches which hung down and curved like the handlebars of a bicycle, imparting to the Professor considerable fierceness of aspect. Across his velvet waistcoat lay a golden watch-chain stretched to its utmost, and his fingers flashed with rings. Leopardo sternly studied these evidences of prosperity; and as he gazed, his eyes sunk back defensively into his head until there was nothing left but a black gleam as from two pieces of coal. Ampersand shifted his bulk and leaned forward, interested in this phenomenon, his own eyes emerging from their sockets until they protruded like two marbles. Professor Ampersand intent, was an awe-inspiring spectacle. Leopardo remembered the story of the cobra at the Zoo which had attempted to outstare the Professor, but had lost consciousness in twenty-two seconds. But Leopardo, The World's Greatest Hypnotist, was no mere cobra. He coldly returned his companion's gaze and taking a diamond-studded cigar cutter from his pocket, neatly snipped the end from his cigar. Professor Ampersand's eyeballs sank back slowly where they belonged. He struck a match and offered Leopardo a light.

'You seem to have done well for yourself in life,' said Leopardo. 'I observe every sign of prosperity.'

Ampersand emitted a cloud of smoke from his mouth and nostrils before he replied. 'I have done well, my friend. And you have too.'

'My name is very widely known in Europe and America,' asserted Leopardo. 'I have appeared in the theatres of most capitals. I have demonstrated my art before royalty.'

Though he watched closely, he could detect neither contempt nor disbelief in the Professor's face. The handle-bar moustaches concealed the corners of Ampersand's mouth, and there was nothing to be learnt from his eyes.

'It is good, my friend. In the same walk in life we might have been rivals and injured one another. You went your way, I went mine. For you the glitter of the stage and the applause of thousands, for me the quiet of the consulting room and the knowledge that I am serving humanity.'

A vein started to pulse in Leopardo's temple. 'Mine is the better way,' he said tensely. 'I demonstrate my gifts to the world; you sell yours to the few like a mere doctor.'

Ampersand sat back with a slight air of disapproval. Then he stirred and waved an expansive hand.

'My friend, we fell out over that issue thirty years ago. Don't rake up again the hot words of youth.'

'You were always jealous of my abilities,' hissed Leopardo, his face convulsed with sudden hatred. 'You knew there was no room for two great hypnotists.'

Ampersand's voice was gentle: 'We went different ways. It turned out all for the best.'

'Deny it if you dare. You've always affected to despise me. You pretend to yourself that my stage shows are the vulgarisation of a great profession. That's what you said thirty years ago.'

'Thirty years ago,' repeated Ampersand, sadly. 'My friend . . . '

'Don't call me your friend. Do you want to drive me mad?'

The Professor let his hands fall with an air of hopelessness on to his two plump knees. 'You are overwrought,' he said sternly. 'Calm down.'

He arose, sighed gloomily and wandered across the room. He stood for a moment with his back turned, stroking his square jaw. When he turned again, he saw that Leopardo had buried his face in his hands. Ampersand seated himself once more, relit his cigar and waited. When Leopardo uncovered his face, it was strained, and terror and pathos showed in his dark eyes.

'What do you want me to do?' asked Ampersand quietly. 'I assure you that I'll help you in any way I can.'

Leopardo did not speak until his face had resumed its usual immobility. 'I'm sorry for my outburst,' he said at last. 'I'm very unwell.'

Ampersand leaned forward, his elbow resting on his knee, and pointed his cigar at his companion. 'How unwell?' he demanded.

'I've lost the ability to sleep. I'm physically exhausted. I've gone for ten days and nights in dread that I should have caused the deaths of many thousand people.'

'Did they die?'

'No. For ten days and nights I've worked as no man has ever worked before. I've saved them all, every one.'

'Then why are you worrying?'

'I wish you wouldn't keep stabbing questions at me with that cigar.' There was a fresh note of hysteria in Leopardo's voice, and Professor Ampersand immediately jerked the cigar into the fireplace and sank back into his chair where he sat brooding into his moustache.

When Leopardo again spoke, his voice was under control. 'My nerves are completely shattered,' he said. 'I'm a mentally sick man, and as I don't believe in doctors, I've come to one of my own profession. Hypnosis may cure me; nothing else will.'

Professor Ampersand brooded even more deeply.

'You want me to treat you?' he asked at last.

'Yes, if you will.'

It was some time before the Professor raised his chin from out of his velvet waistcoat.

'I'll do it, of course,' he said heavily, 'but it will be a difficult operation. Your will is probably as strong as my own, and I don't doubt that it will unconsciously resist me. I shall first induce hypnotic slumber; and when you are asleep, I shall, by suggestion, purge your mind of its terrors; but to do so, I must first understand what those terrors are, so I must ask you to relate to me all the happenings since your radio broadcast of two weeks ago. I read the newspapers, and I'm therefore generally familiar with what has occurred, but I should prefer to hear it all from your own lips. I should mention that I'm something of a psycho-analyst as well as a hypnotist, so that I attach importance to the principle of self-confession.'

'Have you ever treated a case like mine?'

'No, I don't think so; but I've had considerable success in alleviating neuralgia and rheumatic pains, headaches and dyspepsia. Yes, and even functional paralysis. In one sitting I cured an atrocious dipsomaniac by filling him with beneficial suggestions. He has since made a fortune running a

99

mineral water factory. Relax now and relate to me all that has occurred.'

'It all began,' said Leopardo, 'with that unfortunate broadcast last Monday week. I was approached by the radio authorities with the suggestion that I should give a demonstration of my skill over the air. The broadcast was successful, unfortunately only too successful. I was awakened in my bed at the hotel the following morning by an inspector of police who thrust a newspaper into my hand. I could scarcely believe the headlines. Listeners to my broadcast in every part of the country were frozen rigid in hypnotic slumber and defied all efforts to awaken them. Already over two thousand cases had been reported. In houses everywhere people were standing and sitting like statues, some at the tea-table with cups of tea suspended in the air and even with bits of bread-and-butter half-way down their throats. One impossible man who had brought the wireless set into the bathroom with him while he was shaving, was standing there stiff as a board with an open razor pressed so hard against his jugular vein that his relatives were afraid to move him.'

'It was a great triumph for the profession,' commented Ampersand meditatively, 'but of course, it was very embarrassing for you.'

'It was terrible,' continued Leopardo with a break in his voice. 'I immediately placed myself at the disposal of the authorities. First, I gave a counter-broadcast in an attempt to de-hypnotise those that were affected, but it seems that relatively few came out of their trance. At all events, the official reports that evening showed that there were still no less than four thousand and thirty-two persons in every part of the country in a state of suspended mobility.'

'Hm!' grunted the Professor, as from under his beetling brows he studied the nervously-twitching face of his companion.

'It was terrible. Those four thousand and thirty-two persons had to be reanimated before they died of starvation. How was I to do it?'

There was terror in Leopardo's eyes as he raised them beseechingly to the florid face of the Professor. Ampersand's great forehead contracted in a frown, and he seemed to bend his will-power on his fellow hypnotist. Leopardo's hand which had been fluttering in nervous gestures, grew still; and he laid it on the arm-rest of his chair.

'Pull yourself together,' commanded Ampersand. 'After all, you succeeded.'

'I'll admit the police organised things very well. All over the country people were instructed to convey the afflicted into the county towns. Halls were everywhere requisitioned; and the hypnotised . . . men, women and children, even household pets, dogs and cats, were packed into the halls in rows, each subject at a distance of two feet from its neighbour. Then started my nightmare tour: from town to town, from hall to hall I went, under heavy police escort to protect me from the angry mobs, de-hypnotising them in hundreds. Can you imagine the sights that confronted my eyes as I stood on the platforms of those shabby little halls, packed full with living statues, but with no more movement in them than if they were dead, long rows of them with their blank faces turned towards me? Old and young there were, in every sort of grotesque pose. There'd be a young man with a glass of beer jammed to his lips, and two feet away from him a water spaniel with its muzzle raised in the air; then an old woman with her knitting. The man with the razor pressed against his jugular vein, was conveyed into town by his relatives in a crate, packed in sawdust and wood shavings. I had to do a special job on him; and his wife, instead of being grateful, aimed a blow at me with her umbrella. And all the time there was the gnawing fear that someone had been left behind. How do I know yet that many may not have been . . . mountainy farmers in remote cottages frozen immobile in their kitchens until they are found in a year or two perhaps, crumbled into dust, their naked skulls still inclined towards the wireless set which will play on for months to come in that terrible silence; lovers in motor-cars in lonely laneways who happened to switch on their sets the moment before I started that unfortunate broadcast? How am I to know that it's all over yet? Maybe there are still many in hypnotic trance in every corner up and down the land. How can we know . . . ?'

Professor Ampersand watched the beads of sweat emerging from the roots of Leopardo's hair and slowly moving down his forehead.

'Idle fears,' asserted the Professor. 'You did your best. No blame attaches to you. Idle fears.'

'I feel the weight of responsibility . . . ' began Leopardo.

'I'm not starting an argument,' snapped the Professor. 'I'm insinuating healthy thoughts into your psyche. Kindly do not interrupt me.'

He arose and prowled up and down behind Leopardo's chair.

'Idle fears,' he enunciated with a dreamy persuasiveness. 'Idle fears. Your conscience is clear. Let that thought penetrate your inmost being. You . . . are . . . not . . . to . . . blame. Idle fears.'

Leopardo looked up at him. 'You'll have to try something stronger than that baby stuff to do any good with me.'

'Idle fears,' repeated the Professor with a rising note of anger in his voice. 'Kindly stand up, look into my eyes and fix your attention on me.'

Leopardo did as he was bid, taking his stand in the middle of the carpet about six feet from the Professor.

'Idle fears. Lay open your soul so that my will may penetrate it, and purge it of all those idle fears, so that it may be washed clean, washed of all its idle fears, those idle, idle fears.'

Leopardo drew a handkerchief from his pocket and blew his nose.

'Idle fears,' repeated the Professor savagely. 'I can do nothing for you if you resist my will. Idle fears. Make blank your mind, let your will sag so that I may bend it to my own, purging it clean, purging it clean of its idle fears.'

The Professor raised his hand and began a series of sleep-inducing passes before Leopardo's face, then he leaned to one side, seemed to collect a handful of air from somewhere in the neighbourhood of his knee, came back into the upright again, and softly flung the handful of air into Leopardo's face. Then he began to sway slightly, crooning persuasively: 'Idle fears. Idle fears.'

A contemptuous sneer appeared at the corner of Leopardo's mouth. The Professor became still. The veins stood out on his forehead like ropes, as he laboured to concentrate every atom of his mighty will and bring it to bear. His eyeballs protruded, and his terrible gaze drove like a knife into the black depths of Leopardo's eyes. The sneer slowly froze on Leopardo's mouth, and his eyes retracted until they became two glittering pieces of black returning the Professor's fearsome stare. They stood motionless, their wills locked in titanic battle; and in the consulting room there was an unearthly silence.

At nine o'clock the following morning Carruthers, the receptionist, entered and was astonished to find his master and Leopardo standing glaring menacingly into each other's eyes. With a muttered word of apology he closed the door behind him and softly withdrew. He looked in again at eleven and before going to his lunch at one, but found no change in the situation. At three o'clock he became alarmed and tried to awaken the gentlemen by pulling at their coat-tails. At five o'clock he telephoned the police.

Three days later a group of consultant specialists stood in the waiting-room of Number 308, Middleton Square. The City Medical Officer entered from the hall followed by Carruthers looking pale and worried.

'But what about my wages, sir?'

'I wish you wouldn't keep bothering me with these trivialities,' snapped the Medical Officer. 'I told you already that your master is merely in a state of suspended animation, and that as long as he is alive, his estate cannot be touched without an Act of Parliament. Please go away.'

The receptionist retired to the kitchen where he seated himself at the table with his head on his hand.

Doctor Codd emerged from the window embrasure polishing his pince-nez with a silk handkerchief.

'Well,' he said, 'there's nothing further that we can do. We've tried everything. A most remarkable case. Most remarkable. I trust,' he added jocularly, 'that payment of our fees will not also have to await an Act of Parliament.'

'Of course not, gentlemen; the City will look after that.'

The specialists smiled deprecatingly and began to put on their overcoats.

'You tell me,' said Doctor Codd, 'that you have been in touch with every known hypnotist?'

'Yes,' replied the Medical Officer, 'with every single one in this country and with two in Paris. They, one and all, refuse to have anything to do with the case. Naturally, they are afraid to confront Ampersand or Leopardo, lest the same fate should befall themselves.'

'All that can apparently be done,' said Doctor Codd as he shook hands with the Medical Officer, 'is to keep them both alive with food injections administered daily.'

'We'll look after that,' said a tall man of academic aspect.

The group paused in the doorway to watch the two hypnotists being carried down the steps as stiff as boards to the waiting ambulance. Police cleared a way through the gaping crowds, and Ampersand and Leopardo started on their journey to the University Museum and the glass-case which had been prepared for them.

The Metamorphosis of a Licensed Vintner

IT'S A deplorable thing for a man when love comes to him in middle age. Most of us get it over when we're young. We find ourselves married, and we spend the rest of our lives wondering what happened to us. It costs us a lot of money going to cinemas and reading books to try and find out. That's normal; and it's the way things should be; but to see a man that's middle-aged, becoming enmeshed is a most harrowing sight.

I felt the greatest sympathy for John Marcus Whittaker when the bolt struck him, though he got scant pity from the others who gathered every Saturday night in John Marcus's Select Bar—O'Brien the solicitor, Doctor Murphy and the rest. They seemed to think it was the greatest joke that had burst on Caherbeg for many a long day. Of course, in a small town people have very little to talk about, and poor John Marcus Whittaker was wholly incapable of keeping his hopes and fears to himself.

He was forty-five when it happened, a plump man with thinning hair and a face of such innocence that strangers concluded at once that his brain was naturally moist. He stood all day behind the counter in his Select Bar without very much to say for himself, but ready to laugh uproariously at even the feeblest jest. He enjoyed our Saturday evenings to the full—I can see him now leaning across the counter convulsed at the quick backchat between the solicitor and the doctor, while thirsty customers hammered the counter with their empty glasses in a vain attempt to attract his attention. His only amusement was fishing, and like all anglers that are not much good, he was always running into incredible

adventures. I remember the day he brought the old red setter
fishing with him, a harmless, well-meaning dog; and what did
John Marcus do with his first back-cast but hook the unfortunate animal by the tail. The dog didn't stop to ask any
questions, but made a bee-line for home, with John Marcus,
who didn't want to lose a new cast and a length of line,
scampering after him, round trees and over bushes, letting
out the line from his reel as he ran, playing the luckless hound
as if he were a fish. I had a great fondness for John Marcus; so
that when his trouble came on him, I had little inclination to
join in with the others in laughing at the ups and downs of his
love affair.

It all began when John Marcus accepted an invitation to
afternoon tea from Mrs. Bailey, an old lady who lived with
her daughter in one of the new bungalows on the edge of the
town. He described it all to me the next day with what I can
only call bated breath. The old lady had been all dolled up in
black with jet earrings swinging out of her ears and yards of
black beads wound in a string around her neck. She had
talked all the time while her daughter Mabel served the tea
and then sat with a slight smile on her face gazing into the
fire. Mrs. Bailey was a policeman's widow, and accordingly
she had a great respect for the old gentry. When she wasn't
talking about them, she was regaling John Marcus with the
family history of the crowned heads of Europe. The girl
didn't say a word the whole evening except 'How do you do?'
and 'Good-bye'; neither did John Marcus. He sat on the
other side of the fire with a cup of tea balanced on the palm of
his hand and the sweat rolling down his face.

I thought the whole affair had a serious ring, but I wasn't
anxious to jump to conclusions without further evidence.
It was the sort of case where you must just wait and watch.
He had accepted an invitation for the following Sunday as
well (he had been afraid to refuse it), and he promised to

report any further developments. I advised him to say nothing to anyone, and even if the Bailey family was mentioned to him, to deny that he had ever heard of them. But John Marcus, as I said already, was no good at keeping things to himself, and he blurted it all out to the boys in the Select Bar on the following Saturday night. Well, as you know, a sort of bush telegraph operates in small Irish towns, and half-an-hour after John Marcus had admitted that he had been invited to the Bailey household on the previous Sunday, the whole town was buzzing with the news that the old lady was trying to fix a match between John Marcus and the daughter.

My worst fears were confirmed on the following Sunday when John Marcus came up to the house to report to me on the afternoon's happenings. He was out of breath when he arrived, and I could see that he was considerably shaken. When I had put him in the armchair and given him a half-glass of whiskey, he told me the story in a faltering voice. Mabel Bailey had sat by the fire just as on the previous occasion, not saying a word; but he swore that she smiled at him every time he inadvertently caught her eye, which was only three times in the whole course of the afternoon. John Marcus was inclined to think that the smile was more on the left side of her mouth than on the right, but he wasn't quite certain because, as you can well imagine, he had been afraid to look at her. The conversation had been about the great ducal families of England, but two significant things had happened. First, John Marcus had dropped one of the old lady's Crown Derby cups and smashed it, but instead of telling him what she thought of him, Mrs. Bailey had beamed at him benevolently and assured him that she had five more of them in the cupboard. Second, just before he left she had suddenly switched from the ducal families of England to some searching questions as to the progress of his business.

Was it true, she had asked, that he was making money hand over fist? She and the daughter had seen him to the door, but not before they had extorted a promise from him that he would come and visit them again on the following Sunday.

On considering all the facts, I was forced to the conclusion that the old lady was out to trap poor John Marcus; and the daughter was probably acquiescent. I like John Marcus, and I found it hard to break the news to him. I felt guilty when I saw the shadow coming down his face just like when you're pulling down the blind. He reminded me of our long acquaintance and begged for advice. That wasn't easy. It was no use advising him to avoid the house like the plague, because it was obvious that he hadn't the courage to refuse the old lady's invitations; nor could he be expected to sell his business and leave the town. After all, the public house had been in the family for three generations, and anyway John Marcus was used to the people in the town and they were used to him. He wouldn't have done well in business anywhere else. It was a problem. If he went away on a protracted holiday, who was there to look after the business in his absence? All I could advise him to do, was to stand his ground like a man and hope for the best.

To this day, I don't blame Mrs. Bailey. She was advanced in years, and the widow's pension which she enjoyed, was due to die with her. What was more natural than that she should be anxious to see the daughter settled in life and married to a good, solid man? I've nothing against Miss Bailey either. I've never spoken to her, but I'm sure she's a nice girl. She looks it anyway. I've often seen her moving round the town, a graceful girl with a slightly distant look on her face and that slight smile as if she was thinking of far-away things. It was just unfortunate that they picked on John Marcus.

To give him his due, I truly believe that the only emotion which he experienced during his first six weeks' acquaintance with the Baileys, was terror. I think it was that slight smile of Miss Bailey's that finally got him; and one Saturday night in the Select Bar we all suddenly realised that instead of being terrified that Miss Bailey would marry him, he had unaccountably become terrified that she wouldn't.

He began by asking whether it wasn't the case that women had the strongest objection to marrying men whose hair was thin. Poor John Marcus thought he was being terribly subtle, and he kept asking general questions about masculine looks and the prejudices of ladies in the matter, not realising that there wasn't a man in the Select Bar that hadn't his ears cocked. Of course, O'Brien the solicitor led him on; and it wasn't until John Marcus suddenly noticed the gloom on my face, that he realised that he had given away his secret. He became flustered; and in a clumsy attempt to save himself, he blurted out something silly about it being embarrassing to see a girl with a slight smile on her face, and you not to know what she's smiling at. Everyone roared laughing, and poor John Marcus stood there with the blushes creeping up his forehead and in between the roots of his scanty hair. I'll say this for the boys, that once they had wrung an admission from him that he was afraid Miss Bailey was amused at his baldness, and when they had had their laugh, they flung themselves with might and main into the business of helping him. The Doctor insisted that a diet of watercress worked wonders with falling hair, but O'Brien the solicitor waved all such old woman's remedies aside with a gesture of contempt.

'There's only one infallible method of growing hair,' he said. 'Burn the leather of an old boot, powder the ashes, and mix them with fresh lard. Apply the mixture to the skull every night in generous quantities.'

My heart was too full to say anything. I just shook John Marcus by the hand and went home.

Well, it was the queerest situation you ever saw. There was old Mrs. Bailey doing everything in her power to bring John Marcus to the point of proposing to the girl, while he sat there Sunday after Sunday in a lather of perspiration absolutely convinced that Miss Bailey was secretly amused at his middle-aged appearance and his high forehead, and that nothing in the world would persuade her to marry him. And the young lady sat smiling into the fire, not saying a word.

John Marcus tried the old boot and the lard for four days, but he had to give it up because the mixture attracted every fly in the shop on to his head. They even followed him down the street and tried to get in under his hat. The collection of watercress wasn't easy either. You'd see him of an evening scouting along the ditches on the roads outside the town, and searching for pools in low-lying ground. Watercress grows in very wet places, and soon he was complaining of rheumatism in both his knees. Then he tried the marrow from a calf's shin-bone, applied night and morning and well rubbed in, but that didn't do any good either. He tried every bottle of guaranteed hairgrower in the chemist's shop, but the only result was that his scalp turned pink. A travelling salesman tried to sell him a bottle of 'Hairo' and swore black and blue that he had spilt a bottle of it on the linoleum in his own house and in the morning there was a rug there, but John Marcus wasn't as simple as that. He had almost despaired of winning Miss Bailey's affections when one evening the Doctor walked into the Select Bar and pointed to an advertisement in a Dublin newspaper which he held in his hand. John Marcus clutched desperately at the paper like a drowning man.

'Giuseppe Tromboni?' he read, 'Master Trichologist, late of London and Milan, guarantees to grow hair in three weeks. Consultations by appointment only.'

'Do you think there's anything in it?' asked John Marcus.

'Well, you can try,' replied the Doctor. 'Tho' what you're worrying about beats me. You've got plenty of hair at the sides and quite a bit at the front.'

'It's the sort of tonsure I have on the top, that has me worried,' said John Marcus. 'Anyway, the bald area is spreading.'

'No wonder,' retorted the Doctor, 'with all the queer things you've been rubbing into it. If you had only stuck to the watercress, you'd at least have strengthened the fibres of what you have.'

'It's all very well to talk,' replied John Marcus gloomily. 'You'd need to be a rabbit to subsist entirely on a diet of greens. Besides I've eaten up all the watercress that grows for miles around.'

I walked with him to the station on the day appointed for his interview with Signor Tromboni. As he stepped out gaily, his face bright with hope, he rallied me gently about my moodiness.

'I was born a diffident man,' he explained, 'but if I could only get enough hair to grow to cover the bald patch, it would give me courage. No matter what you all say, I can't get it out of my head that she thinks I'm funny-looking; so that every time she looks at me, I feel the joints of my knees giving away, and I expect to fall on the floor. But this foreign expert will make a new man of me, and with Mrs. Bailey on my side, as you all seem to think she is, I'll sweep the daughter off her feet.'

'I hope it's all for the best,' I said heavily.

'Of course it is,' he responded heartily. 'Cheer up, man, and don't be looking so mournful.'

He waved a plump white hand to me from the carriage window as the train moved out of the station, and I walked slowly to the house to await the outcome.

John Marcus was surprised to find that the Master Trichologist had set up his consulting rooms in one of the poorer streets of the city. The waiting-room was hung with pictures of gentlemen before and after they had passed through Signor Tromboni's hands, the first of each pair of photographs showing skulls of horrible nudity or at best with a few unhealthy bunches of thatch, while the second showed the same gentlemen with an incredible, luxurious growth. John Marcus walked round the room studying with considerable satisfaction these evidences of Signor Tromboni's ability, and he was particularly impressed by a large framed certificate from an English College of Trichologists which announced that Signor Giuseppe Tromboni had graduated with First Class Honours.

Before long the door of the inner sanctum was flung open, and the Master Trichologist himself stood in the doorway smiling affably at John Marcus. He was a big, impressive man, and by way of compensation for his own lack of hair his face was draped with a heavy black moustache. He courteously invited John Marcus to enter and waved him into a barber's chair in front of a basin and mirror. Then he brought a powerful lamp into position over John Marcus's head, and picking up an enormous magnifying glass he began his examination. John Marcus was distressed to hear him groaning aloud once or twice, and to see him in the mirror shaking his head despondently. Then he put his lamp and magnifying glass aside, and gripping John Marcus firmly by the base of the skull, he pulled out a small handful of hair, which he stowed away carefully in an envelope.

'We must send it to London for analysis,' he explained gravely, 'so that we may learn the extent to which it is diseased. Come back to me in a week. That'll be a guinea.'

John Marcus paid up, shook hands and found himself in the street, marvelling at the foreign gentleman's command of English and the speed with which he had acquired a Dublin accent.

On the occasion of John Marcus's next visit, Signor Tromboni congratulated him and told him that the report from London had been promising, but that the course of treatment which he would recommend, would be long and expensive. When John Marcus replied that he didn't mind the expense, the Master Trichologist rubbed his hands with satisfaction and indicated his readiness to commence Course No. 1 forthwith.

Course No. 1 was electrical treatment. John Marcus was clamped in a chair and electrical charges passed through his skull so as to stimulate the roots of his hair, but the patient's reflexes got out of control, and Signor Tromboni abandoned the treatment with regret after receiving two kicks in the stomach. When the electricity was switched off, John Marcus was found to be in a semi-paralysed condition, and assistance had to be summoned to get him out of the chair, into his overcoat, and through the doorway on to the street.

John Marcus was then subjected to Course No. 2 three days a week for a month. Signor Tromboni began by plunging the patient's head into a basin of near-boiling water so as to open the pores; and when the pores were thoroughly opened, he dragged John Marcus back into the chair and rubbed powerful ointments into his scalp. Then before John Marcus could recover his breath, his head was seized and plunged into freezing water so as to close the pores before the ointment could get out. As a side-line the Trichologist sold John Marcus various wire brushes and combs, and a half-dozen bottles of hair stimulant. When this had gone on for four weeks, John Marcus protested that he thought the violence of the treatment was injuring his heart. Signor Tromboni, after a prolonged scrutiny with the magnifying glass, ruefully admitted that he couldn't see any fresh hair coming up. He consented to put John Marcus through Course No. 3.

What the unfortunate man endured passes all belief. Expenses were mounting, and John Marcus was beginning to think that he'd have to take out a mortgage on the business. A course of ultraviolet ray treatment which followed, was unproductive of result. The Master Trichologist was becoming more and more exasperated at the failure of fresh hair to sprout. He seemed to think that his professional honour was at stake, and his handling of John Marcus's head became extremely rough. At last one day his exasperation overcame him. He flung his magnifying glass into a corner of the room and fixed John Marcus with a piercing eye.

'Do you really want your hair to grow?' he demanded.

'Yes,' faltered John Marcus watching him nervously.

Signor Tromboni turned sharply and going to a press in the corner, unlocked it with a long, shining key. He came back with a bottle in his hand.

'This will either kill or cure,' he asserted. 'Will you take it?'

John Marcus hesitated. He didn't like the glint in the Master Trichologist's eye, but he thought of Miss Bailey, and he put out his hand for the bottle.

'Apply to-night before retiring,' said Signor Tromboni, 'and rub well in.'

He saw John Marcus to the door and shook him by the hand.

John Marcus did as he was bid. The mixture smelt of gunpowder, but he rubbed it in doggedly. He was conscious of a burning sensation, and when he went to bed, he slumbered fitfully. In the morning when he ran the comb through his hair in front of the glass, all the hair he had came off on the comb.

I've always said it's a terrible thing when love comes to a

man in middle-age. John Marcus never went to the Bailey household again; in fact, he didn't go out-of-doors at all for two years. He has grown fat and puffy, and his head is as bald as an egg. He applied himself assiduously to his business. He bought two other public houses and extended the Select Bar round the corner. He opened a grocery and evicted a family of orphans so as to make room for his new Ice Cream Emporium. He never serves in the Select Bar himself now; instead there are two whippersnappers in white coats anticipating your slightest wish, and moving round noiselessly against a background of chromium and red leather seats. John Marcus is Chairman of the Town Commissioners and a director of the new factory. In short, he has become what they call 'one of the most respected citizens of the town'.

I saw Miss Bailey the other day as she was coming out of the greengrocer's with a bundle of rhubarb under her arm. She was lightly swinging a shopping basket, and she passed me with that same slight smile upon her face.